DRAWN TO THE DEMON DUKE

INTERNATIONAL BESTSELLING AUTHOR
SARAH SPADE

Cover by Fran of Merry-Book-Round

Interior Art by JoY Design Studio

Illustration by Ale of Magik4le

FOREWORD

Thank you for checking out *Drawn to the Demon Duke*!

I just want to point out that, though this novella is technically a prequel—as it's set in the late 1980s and is the the first in the series chronologically—I highly recommend that this story be read at the conclusion of the series to avoid certain spoilers.

When I was plotting the complete series back around book three, it became clear to me that Susanna was more than the character who cast the matefinder spell in the first place. Yes, she was also Amy's aunt *and* Haures's mate, but with the doppelseers' prophecy becoming the overarching plot to tie up the end of the series, I realized that Susanna was just as involved in it as Shannon and Malphas.

Because of that, I decided to wait to release her story until that part was revealed in the final book in the main series, *Shannon in Sombra.* And while this novella spends the majority of the book focusing on how Haures and Susanna met, and why she chose to stay with the fearsome demon duke, the epilogue is set after *Shannon in Sombra* so there will be spoilers for that book there.

This story will also answer plenty of questions. Did you ever wonder how Susanna got the book in the first place? How did she end up with Dagon as a devoted guard until he found his HEA with Sierra? And what about her trip into the shadows to find the ashbalm flower? All that—and more—is finally answered in *Drawn to the Demon Duke.*

So, in short, please note that this is a prequel novella, set before *Mated to the Monster*, with Duke Haures as the lead (which means that a lot of established rules are different here because of his unique status/abilities). It absolutely relies on the fated mates/instalove trope, with a heroine who actually *wants* to be whisked away by a demon, the demon duke who appears both hot and cold until you discover that two thousand years of being the outcast with the crown has messed him up good, and a HEA that spans more than forty years… so far.

So have fun with the 1980s references, and enjoy watching as Susanna realizes that Haures is her true love—and what exactly that means for the two of them.

xoxo,

Sarah

CHAPTER 1
SHE'S A LITTLE RUNAWAY

SUSANNA

Twining my finger around the coils of the phone cord, absently watching through my window, I'm barely paying attention to my older sister as she's telling me about the Bon Jovi and Skid Row concert she went to last weekend with her husband, Dan, and some of their friends over at the Hartford Civic Center.

Mindy is ten years older than I am. Thirty-eight to my twenty-eight, she's been like my second mom for as long as I can remember. Even after she had her own daughter a little over eight years ago, Mindy still can't help but mother me. Considering she and Amy are the only family I have left, I usually take it with a grain of salt.

But not today.

"They even sang 'Runaway'," Mindy adds, and that little jab has my attention snapping from the window, frowning as I grip the phone handle with my other hand.

"C'mon, Min. I didn't run away," I begin, the same old refrain to a tired song. "The house in Madison was going for a good price. I couldn't live with you and Dan forever."

Sometimes I think Mindy would've preferred that I did. She was happy to take me in after Mom died during my senior year of high school, and with Dad having pulled a runaway stunt of his own when I was fourteen, my sister was all I had.

My sister—and my book.

The book that's been part of my life for so long that, to me, it's part of my family… and, to Mindy, the reason she wanted to keep me under her nose for as long as she could…

But while I did stay with my sister's family for a couple of years, earning my keep by helping with the baby after Mindy had Amy, *I* knew I couldn't stay. The small inheritance I got from Mom's passing was enough for a down payment, and the realtor I worked with suggested this one in Madison. Sure, it was farther from Mindy than she liked, but I got a solid job at the call center, I attend aerobics classes every Tuesday and Thursday to keep fit, and if I'm still single as I'm creeping up on thirty, it doesn't bother me half as much as it does my older sister.

"I know," she concedes, and if she gives in too easily about my having moved out four years ago, it's only because she has bigger fish to fry. "Jeff missed you. He thought you'd be at the concert. Seemed real disappointed that Dan brought his cousin instead."

I roll my eyes. "I was busy."

"I know. That's what you told me when I asked if you'd babysit Amy."

Huffing, I turn slightly, tugging on the coils. "I promised Lissy that I'd have dinner after our shift was done."

Even through the phone, I swear I can just hear the way Mindy arches her eyebrow in disbelief. "And that's all you did? You didn't spend last Friday with your nose in a book, did you?"

A book, she says. What Mindy really means is *that* book.

Of course she does.

I sigh, scratching my ankle with the heel of my sneaker, scrunching my neon pink leg warmer. After I left the call center earlier this afternoon, I popped some bagel bites into the toaster oven, then got ready for tonight's Tuesday aerobics class. My hair is in its usual side pony, my leg warmers slouched down over my leggings, with the slightly oversized t-shirt a matching shade of pink covering up my navy sports bra. I was just getting ready to head out when the phone rang, and now I've been talking to Mindy for the last fifteen minutes.

And, no matter how any conversation begins, it always ends up with Mindy double-checking that I've stopped obsessing over the leather-bound antique of a book I bought at a garage sale when I was sixteen.

So I tell her what she wants to hear because, otherwise, I'll only worry her—and that's the last thing I'd ever want to do if I could avoid it.

"Not Friday. I was getting my Uncle Jesse fix instead."

Mindy chuckles, and I swallow a sound of relief. So she thinks I watch *Full House* on Fridays because I have a crush on John Stamos. It might not be a real man, but I know it makes her feel better that I can be attracted to *any* guy. She's always had Dan. Me? Apart from a few stolen kisses when I was still in school, I'm single and not really ready to mingle.

I don't know why, and I certainly can't explain it to Mindy. I like guys, and I've found plenty of them attractive over the years—even if I can't say the same about Dan's buddy, Jeff—but… crud. It's just never been right.

Like they've never been 'the one'.

That, at least, is one thing that Mindy can't blame on the book. Instead, she points out that if I stopped crushing on fictional characters—like Uncle Jesse or Jareth the Goblin King or Sam from *Cheers*—maybe I could find my own happily-ever-after with a real-life man.

Really? How boring would *that* be?

I don't want boring. I don't want ordinary.

I want something *more*, and if it's because I've spent most of my formative years convinced that I can find it in a centuries-old spellbook, well… what Mindy doesn't know won't hurt her. Besides, she has her own family to take care of. Dan and Amy should be her focus. Me? I'm doing okay.

And I'm about to try to convince her of that for the millionth time when I catch sight of the mailman walking jauntily toward my front door, and I'm suddenly doing *better*.

"Mindy? I gotta go."

"Su—"

"Mailman's at the door." I wait for the *knock*, grinning when I hear it. "I should answer it."

"Don't you want to say 'hi' to Amy?"

I love my niece. I really do. She's a precocious, sweet eight-year-old who is the spitting image of us Benoit women. Even though Mindy is Mindy Dillon now after marrying Dan, the Benoit genes rang true in her little girl. Amy has our same dark eyes and dark brown hair, and an expression that says she's always a little dreamy. The hardest part of moving out was not being able to see her every day, but I needed to do it.

I needed to work toward *my* future.

"Tell her I love her, would you, Min? And I'll call back after aerobics. 'Kay? Love you!"

Unraveling myself from the twist of the phone cord, I place the handle on the receiver on the wall before Mindy can respond. Then, trying to fight against my giddy hope in case I'm wrong, I hurry for the door.

For weeks now, I've gotten an irrational thrill every single time my mail is delivered. I'm so, so close… all I needed was a little reassurance that I'm on the right track, but it's been ages since I wrote my letter, requesting a response. I'm too stubborn to believe that he won't write back. After all, over the years, I've written countless letters—to priests and scholars, self-proclaimed witches and some Satanists—and nearly all of them answered me and my questions.

The way I see it, if the books in the library can't help me, there has to be someone who can. Once I had my own place, I signed up for every magazine on the occult that I could. Between them and the phone book, there were so many experts I could write to, and now that I'm so friggin' close…

I yank the door open to find that Fenton is still waiting on the porch, a letter in hand.

"For you, Ms. Susanna. Found it stuck at the bottom of my bag. Thought I should deliver it in case it's important. Like the gas bill, you know?"

Oh, please don't be my gas bill… "Thank you, Fenton. I really appreciate it."

I hold out my hand.

He hesitates, and if his eyes travel the length of my tight leggings, I pretend not to notice.

Fenton clears his throat. "Anyway, I was thinking… if you're not doing anything tonight, maybe I could take you out. There's this great bowling alley that opened up on the other end of my route—"

"Maybe some other time," I tell him, hoping I'm not being too brusque. I give my ankle a shake, only realizing that my attempt to draw attention to my leg warmer only made it so that he could openly ogle my lower leg. "Got aerobics tonight."

He nods. "Gotta jazzercise. I understand."

Right. "So… my letter?"

Fenton blinks, then starts, as though remembering the reason he used to come back to my house after he finished his route while I was at work. "Oh, yes. Of course." He holds it out. "Here you go."

I all but snatch it from his grip. "Thanks, Fenton. See you around!"

"Ms. Su—"

Just like I did with Mindy, I end the conversation before he can continue. In this case, I wave again, flash him a smile, then close the door in his face.

I forget all about Fenton once I flip the envelope and see the name scrawled in script on the upper left corner. Mr. Ed Woodrow.

Yes!

Ed Woodrow is the leading demonologist and paranormal expert on the East Coast. He, along with his wife and partner, Lucy, is renowned for visiting haunted houses, but that's not all. With the Satanic Panic on late-night news and the front page of all the papers, Mr. Woodrow's gone on lecturing tours, discussing that the barbaric Satanic rituals invented by the press aren't real—but that demons and ghosts and poltergeists are.

Up until two years ago, I would've claimed that none of it was. But after more than a decade of code-breaking and working toward translating an alien language that doesn't exist in any of the library books I've checked out—and that number is in the *hundreds* —I finally figured it out. I found the key to understanding the book when I realized that while some of the words were derived from romance languages, all the way back to Latin, the rest were basically gibberish. They made no sense, and if they made no sense, I didn't need to know what they said.

Between the Latin, Spanish, French, Italian, and Portuguese dictionaries I bought at B. Dalton's, I was able to find a matching translation for approximately eighty percent of the words in my book.

The *Grimoire du Sombra.*

A *spellbook.*

I knew it. From the moment my fingers brushed against the pitted leather with the pentacle embossed on the cover while combing through a pile of books on the table outside my former neighbor's house, I knew there was something different about it. Something unique. The name on the title page was my first clue that it was something special. Then there was the way it was printed. It was unlike any typeface I'd ever seen, on yellowed pages that were so old, it was basically ancient.

Still, I offered Mrs. Green ten bucks for it—all of my babysitting money from when I watched her kids the Saturday night before—and she let me have it. Little Bobby eventually told me that his mom mentioned not having any idea where the book came from in the first place, but I still thought it was an amazing deal, even if I couldn't read it.

For the next twelve years, I've made it my mission to translate it. Once I knew that I just had to go word by word, I made some progress. I kept a second notebook for my translations, not sure if I was wasting my time, though it felt… *right* to go through the book, page by page.

Until the beginning of summer, when I reached one of the middle pages, and everything changed.

CHAPTER 2
MANIFEST AND PROMISE

SUSANNA

VERUS AMOR.

That's what the blocky print at the top of the page reads. It was easy to translate it since neither of the words was that unfamiliar gibberish, and when I realized it said 'true love', I was stunned.

Stunned and, well, kind of psyched.

A true love spell… is that why this book called to me? Because it knew that innocent sixteen-year-old Suzy Benoit would turn into awkward-in-love twenty-eight-year-old Susanna? That, after a life of reading about and watching love stories with guaranteed happily-ever-afters, I would see a true love spell and believe it could be my only chance at having a happy ending of my own?

Maybe. All I can say for sure is that, for weeks,

I've focused on translating as much of that page as I could in between work and my other responsibilities. It took forever. Of all the pages, it had the most words, broken down into two distinct sections. Following the same scheme, I'd say I was able to translate about eighty-two-ish percent into English; the rest were a collection of harsh syllables that I only hoped didn't change my interpretation of it too much.

Because the spell? I'm pretty sure I understand the difference between the two parts.

The first paragraph had phrases like *the God grant you to your heart* and *I'm calling you,* uxor *my, to me*. I don't know what 'uxor' means exactly, though the rest of the paragraph makes it obvious it's referring to the true love it's trying to call.

No. Manifest. That's the word I jotted down in pencil next to the first paragraph. It's a spell to manifest the true love.

The second paragraph was much longer, repeating that same word, but it's full of promises. Like a wedding vow, almost, and I guess that makes sense. Wouldn't you want to promise that you'd always choose your true love? So though I kept my attempts at the translations in my notebook, once I was sure that I understood what the second paragraph meant, I added the word 'promise' in pencil.

At the top, I doodled 'true love' next to the blocky print so that I knew this page was different from all the others. Those three lines were the only ways I altered the book… except for scribbling my name on the inner cover years ago when I was first afraid Mindy might take it to keep me from devoting all of my time and effort on it… until now.

After I tore open Ed's letter, reading the advice he provided—advice that I wanted confirmation on—I ran to my bedroom, retrieving the book. Still clutching the letter, I tucked the book under my arm, then snagged a pencil.

From the moment I realized that this book was a bona fide spellbook, I always knew that I would read one of the spells. What's the point of owning a grimoire if I didn't at least *try* to do some magic?

I blame my fascination with the book on seeing *Bedknobs and Broomsticks* at an impressionable age. I was only thirteen when the Disney movie came out, and I thought it was magical, the way they had cartoons and people in the same film. Then there was how Eglentine had a magic book and… yeah. Part of me always thought that magic could be real, and not only because I grew up on *Bewitched* reruns.

But, well, Satanic Panic is also a thing. There were enough clues throughout my years-long project of translating the pages to tell me that what I manifest might not be, well, human. That doesn't mean I expect, like, ALF to appear in my house, or maybe even E.T. But what if I pull a Sarah from *Labyrinth* and manifest a goblin king into my non-existent brother's bedroom? Or the Lord of Darkness from *Legend*?

Now, I wouldn't complain if David Bowie showed up at my house. But a red-skinned demon with horns? I figured it couldn't hurt to get a little advice from someone who knows what they're doing.

Thank you, Mr. Woodrow.

Cracking the book open, setting his letter down on the left page, I try not to think about my sister. Mindy would be so disappointed if she knew that I was still obsessed with the book. Four years ago, when I came to live in Madison and first got my job at the call center, I fibbed a little and told her that I'd finally realized that I needed to grow up and move on from it.

I didn't. I just got better at not letting anyone know that I dedicated most of my teens and all of my twenties to trying to understand the hold it has on me.

True love. It would be worth it all if I could find my true love.

I was cautious, though. When I wrote to Mr. Woodrow, I asked if there were any precautions I should take if I planned on trying to manifest something into our world. Instead of writing me off as another cuckoo fan, he actually answered me.

Scanning his letter again, I note the things he told me I would need. Chalk… salt… I figured as much and already bought a pack of yellow chalk at Woolworth's. I've got plenty of salt in the kitchen, too. He says I should use the chalk to draw a pentacle, then circle it with the salt. He was even so helpful as to illustrate what he means, and I quickly copy the diagram onto the *verus amor* page to practice it myself before adding a small note to draw it in yellow chalk, then circling it with the salt so I don't forget.

Then, with a hint of a smile on my face, I add a few more instructions. To perform the spell, according to two of the witches I wrote to last month, I'd need an open mind, an open space, a clear floor, and a willingness to be love. The clear floor makes sense now that Mr. Woodrow confirmed I need it for the protective circle, and the willingness to be loved… well, I have to believe in true love if I want the spell to work —and I do. I totally do.

I'll have to write a thank-you note to Mr. Woodrow for his help. For now, I fold up his letter, tucking it into my kitchen drawer as I go to retrieve the salt and the chalk, then get to work on prepping the space for the manifestation.

Sorry, aerobics class. I'm taking tonight off.

I'm a bit of a perfectionist. It takes me three tries with the chalk and the salt before I'm satisfied that it matches the design in Mr. Woodrow's letter. Just in case, I want to protect myself because getting caught up with the occult after Mindy told me not to... not cool, dude. Not cool at all.

I don't doubt that it'll work. It *has* to. I put too much time, too much hope, too much effort into the *Grimoire du Sombra*, and if I get a true love out of it, it'll all be worth it. And if my translation was way off due to those unfamiliar words... at least I have the protective circle to keep me safe.

Once I was done, I thought about grabbing my notebook from my bedroom. In the end, I decided not to. The spell wasn't one hundred percent translated, after all, and if it was written in this language, I'm pretty sure I'm supposed to read it the same way.

So I do. I read the words exactly as they're printed on the page, and I haven't even finished the final syllable when... Yes! Yes! It's happening.

What's happening? I... I don't know. It starts as a white orb that flashes into existence in the center of the protective circle drawn on my wooden floor. It's about the size of a baseball, growing larger and larger, brighter and brighter, until I'm peering at it through slits in my fingers once it's as big as a beach ball.

My room is suddenly inexplicably hot. Humid, too. Sweat beads up along my brow, my ponytail listing as I gasp out a breath. I can't even tell if I'm struggling to breathe at the sudden temperature change—or because the searingly white light of the growing orb *explodes*.

I'm blinded in an instant. Blinking doesn't even

help. All I see is the stunning, shocking brightness, lids closed or not. I rub my eyes, stumbling backward, and when I finally think that I can see again, I open them just enough to see that the orb is… it's *gone.*

More amazingly, there's a… a… *something* standing in the circle, right where the orb was moments ago.

My mouth falls open. One part of me wants to scream. The other part wants to cheer.

Because I did it. I manifested a…

Well, I'm not too sure *what* I manifested besides *massive* and *monster.* Seriously. He—and something about the monster just screams 'he'—is built like a San Francisco 49er. He's huge. Broad shoulders, sculpted muscles, and probably a good two feet taller than me, he's not just huge. He's a *giant.*

He's also as white as the orb that brought him to my house. And not just white, like humans are white. He has white hair with black horns growing out from the top of his head. White tusks jut up from surprisingly lush lips. White, colorless skin, and stark black leather-like pants that—thankfully, or maybe not so thankfully—cover him from the waist down. In fact, the only spot of color aside from black and white on this big guy is his eyes.

They're blue.

A bright, vivid, *glowing* blue.

He snarls something at me in a language I don't understand—but I catch that same word. *Uxor.* No doubt in my mind that he's who I was trying to manifest, but this… demon? Yeah. He totally looks like a demon… this demon with his horns and his tusks and his massive bulk is supposed to be my true love?

Then again, maybe not.

Because while I stare at him, still not sure if I should be afraid or welcoming him to Earth, he gives his head a royal shake. Turning on his heel, clicking the claws I just noticed, he takes a step away from me, and now *he*'s gone.

Gone.

I blink. Like the momentary spell just broke, reality slinks back in, and I'm left with a mess on my floor, my heart pounding, my brain trying to process what in the hell just happened.

I can't. Simple as that. I spent twelve years working toward the moment I could cast one of the old book's spells, and when I did? The demon I summoned took one look at me and left.

Bogus.

Ugh.

Twelve years down the drain in an instant. It didn't matter that I was able to translate thirty-one different spells to some degree. None of them seemed promising. I mean, a spell to compel something called an ungez? Or one to conjure a shadow-breaker? That seemed like it would create a blinding orb, similar to what brought that giant monster into my house, but why bother when I could just flick a light switch?

No. It was like I was inspired to keep going until I

found the true love spell… and when I finally did, the demon took one look at *me* and decided to return to wherever I manifested him from.

Ah, well. Maybe I should've expected something like that. Besides, I can't do anything about it now, and reading the spell a second time only to get rejected again… no, thank you.

Instead, I look at the salt. At the chalk that didn't do anything to contain my manifestation, like Mr. Woodrow claimed it would.

And I sigh.

You know what? I might as well grab a broom. If I can clean this mess up quickly, I might be able to make my aerobics class after all.

CHAPTER 3
SUMMONED

HAURES

"The ash farmers are behind on their quota of grain this cycle."

Caim, head of the Dunkel village, is staring down his long nose at Orias, golden eyes blazing at the male with the twisted horn as he accuses him of reneging on a trade deal.

Orias might have a twisted horn, but it's the mark of a battle against a lesser demon that he won. If a challenge broke out between the two village leaders, I'd lay my coin down that Orias would use his slimmer build to his advantage, barreling into Caim horn-first, then using horns and claws to defeat him.

After all, that's what he did when a rogue soldier targeted an unmated demoness in Chaleur. Orias protected his villager, as any demon in power ought to, and he defeated Yuul. I'm glad he did. If not, I would've had the soldier brought in front of my throne and made an example of to the rest of my realm.

Mates are a sacred thing. The gods grant us forever to find our one true mate, but should we decide to accept any demoness as our lifelong partner, a Sombra demon can—so long as the demoness accepts a male's essence and offers hers—and the mate's promise—in return.

Taking a female because you've tired of waiting? There's a reason some of my people will walk into the shadows at the edge of Sombra, never to return, when the long wait to discover their mate leads them to choose an end to their existence over continued loneliness. Allowing the shadows to take them is the only option for an honorable male.

For a dishonorable male? Death is the only outcome.

But a quarrel over a trade between two local villages? Alas, that is one of the many tedious arguments brought to my castle in Mavro, dropped in my lap as I lean back into my throne, legs spread, crystal crown weighing more heavily at times like these than others.

I am Haures. Duke of Sombra, Lord of the Shadows, Ruler of the Flames.

And today?

I am Haures, arbitrator of silly little disagreements, while I grit my teeth, silently gnashing my tusks as Orias jabs Caim in his unmarked chest.

Ah. That would explain it. Orias's silvery ink stands out against his solid red form; he has four characters etched into his chest, **J-A-H-I**, for his bonded mate. Caim, on the other claw, is without a demoness to call his own, and his aggressive posturing has more to do with jealousy than his pristine horns.

I stay silent, letting the other village leader speak.

"That's only because there is a clan of yillurim that are nesting in the southern fields," Orias retorts.

"So send a hunter to clear the fields."

"Our hunters are protecting Chaleur from a huigitz."

Caim sniffs. "Huigitz are easily tamed. Send a pair of hunters after the beast, and leave the rest to root out the yillurim."

"We've lost three of our best hunters to the shadows and the predator. Relying on a pair would be needless death."

"Dunkel needs its grain."

Orias jabs Caim again. "Then Dunkel can tend to the ash fields."

"In Chaleur?" Caim turns, facing me. "Your grace, please grant us your wisdom. Should my people have to do the work of his farmers? Or should they…"

Though I've dealt with far more tiresome meetings than this one during my two thousand years on the throne, Caim's voice becomes a whisper in my ears as a pounding sound replaces it. My heart… it thrums. *Beat beat, beat beat.* My pulse thuds. My claws curl.

Snap.

Tug.

Yank.

I rise up to my feet.

Though duke I may be, I am even more powerful for the gift I was born with. As though my mother somehow sacrificed any shadows I was meant to have for a unique gift, I am the only existing bondmaster in all of Sombra.

I can sense bonds. I can recognize them before they exist, and in rare situations, I can sever them. The latter is how I took the throne after Yelios abandoned it all those years ago. The demons of that age might've been terrified of my colorless appearance, going so far as to throw me to the shadows and hope they would swallow *me* whole, but that was nothing compared to the understanding that I could rip their one true mate from them should I choose to.

So the bondmaster became duke, because even terrified demons would rebel should I proclaim myself king. I still wear the crown. I still claim the throne. I still lord over Sombra from the capital I built from scratch in Mavro… and, despite how hard I've worked to ignore the bonds existing around me, there are times when the magic plucks at my shadowless skin.

It does so now, but in a way I've never known before. At least, not to this extreme.

Once I followed the doppelseers' lead and agreed to go for the throne, I developed a thin bond with every one of my people. This? They are echoes compared to the strength of the bond pulling me forward.

Because this bond?

It's *mine.*

At last, the one true mate foreseen by the powerful twin seers is calling me to her.

And I must answer.

As a bondmaster, I can travel to any of my subjects in need. Thankfully, the ordinary demon in Sombra has no idea that it is possible to summon their duke to their side. Only Damien and Lucian do it frequently, while a handful of high-ranking clan leaders have that honor.

If I need to travel without relying on a bond, I have Sammael at the ready to use his mage abilities to rip open a portal. That's why, as the strange, glowing portal appears in my throne room, Glaine—the head of my guard, and one of two soldiers flanking my throne during my meetings with my subjects—immediately barks at Sammael for disrupting the meet. But it wasn't Sammael conjuring the portal.

It was the matefinder spell.

Two thousand years ago, the doppelseers told me that my fate was to bond with a mortal female from the legendary human world. However, that wasn't the only prophecy they shared with me when they suggested I succeed Yelios…

A child born of two worlds,
belonging in both, belonging to none,
will bring with them rain,
and the fires of Sombra will be forever done.

That day, when I initially learned of Sombra's fate eventually being placed at the feet of a half-demon, half-human spawn, the first law was born. Once I was Duke Haures, I decreed that there would be no contact with the mortals in their realm. The only exception, of course, would be if the mortal were a Sombra demon's mate calling them. Otherwise, our worlds must be kept separate to save the doppelseers' prophecy from coming to pass before we are ready.

As ruler of Sombra, I can sense it when any of my people go off-plane; as a bondmaster, I can tell when it's due to a mate-induced summoning. The humans wouldn't be able to summon a demon mate without the matefinder spell, but since Fate said that a mortal female would be mine, I agreed with Lucian that we should send the matefinder spell across the veil, charmed to find only a mortal destined to belong to one of my demons.

For two thousand years, we waited. Over the centuries, six different grimoires were bound and passed through a portal into the human world; Damien could sense when one was nothing but dust or ash or debris, leading us to create another so that only a single *Grimoire du Sombra* was on Earth at any given time.

But though we've bound six of the books, there has never been a female mortal who has summoned a Sombran demon to be her mate.

Is that why the legend of the human female has grown? Perhaps. My demons have been satisfied over the centuries, finding their mates in demonesses from nearby realms such as Brille Rouge and Soleil, but I know that some wonder if a mythical human mate might someday summon *him*.

I knew my fate was to bond one of the creatures to me. I just never expected that I'd be the *first*. If Lucian and Damien expected as such, I'd hope they would've warned me, but it doesn't matter.

Leaving the bickering village leaders, my stunned guards, and my curious mage behind, I stepped through the portal in my throne room, exiting out into a world of light, of sweetness, of *ice*… of the complete absence of fire.

A shiver runs through me as I land on a dusty sigil

scrawled on a solid floor. In my castle, I keep crystal tiles beneath our feet to unsettle my visitors. Sombra is a world of fire and ash, but Mavro itself is much cooler, with shades of blue—the same color as my strange bondmaster eyes—tinting everything, including my colorless skin. Here? The air is a breeze. Taking a breath is like burning my lungs in a way quite different from the fire pits in Sombra.

I'm used to having mage-powered orbs providing illumination in my castle. In this strange realm, the light is harsh and yellow, but it's easy to see the wee creature looking up at me in… awe. Yes. Smart human. You should be in awe of Duke Haures.

"Are you my female?" I ask her. "My mate? Tilt your chin, human. Let me see you."

She just gawks.

I am used to that. In my entire existence, I haven't seen another demon such as I. All of the Sombran demons have red skin and black shadows; I have neither. But as the legend of Duke Haures grew, the gawking became worried glimpses, then bowing before their liege.

My human does not bow. She stares at me as though she does not understand a word of Sombran.

But of course she doesn't. She must only know human—until I make a conscious decision to accept this obvious bond between us, that is. Only then would she learn about her male, just as I'll know all about my mate.

I have no shadows. I have no true essence, either. I was born an abomination, and only the doppelseers assuring me that my being a bondmaster would overcome all that I lack, allowing me to claim my mate instantly without the gods' interference, led me to hope that, one day, I should find my female.

And now I have.

She is a queer creature. So small. Put beside me, she would barely reach my unmarked chest. No horns to protect her brow. Her skin is pale; not so colorless as I am, but at least she has a reddish tint that I am missing. And her eyes… they are absolutely dim. I might not have any shadows, but this female… she doesn't have any light.

She is mortal. I don't think I understood what that meant until this very moment. She is mortal and easily eliminated.

Unless I take her.

Unless I protect her.

Unless I keep her safe the only way I can until she is ready to also accept her male on the other end of our bond.

And the only way I can do that? Is with a skill that my top mage possesses.

I've relied on the first law to keep the prophecy at bay and my subjects out of another needless war like those Queen Alana and King Yelios waged against other realms. As long as I don't claim the female as my mate straight away, I can use the first law—that no human should know of Sombra without consequences—to banish her right where no demon can threaten my female before she is made immortal.

The way she gawked in surprise… I don't believe that she is happy to have such a beast as her male. It will take wooing and time to convince her that she will be my forever mate, and with there being factions of Sombra who would do *anything* to see Duke Haures relieved of the crystal crown… I can't risk her.

I *won't* risk her.

Promising my female that I will return for her—though she might not be as satisfied as I am with that vow—I use my brand of magic to reopen the summoning portal, placing the other end in my throne room. Stepping inside, I reappear moments after I left.

I've always been led to believe that time runs differently between certain realms. A trip to Soleil might not, but Earth is such a different and strange land compared to Sombra, it could've been mere moments or it could've been entire cycles that passed.

As soon as I return, my feet touching down on the familiar crystal floor of my throne room, I know exactly which.

Orias and Caim are still in Mavro, though their petty argument seems to have been forgotten for the moment. Glaine and Sammael are muttering darkly to each other while Firn is pacing anxiously behind my throne as I approach.

I point a claw at Glaine. "Send a small battalion of soldiers to Chaleur to eliminate the huigitz plaguing their village. Firn? Accompany Caim to Dunkel to assist in clearing out the yillurim. The grains should grow before the next gold moon. The trade bargain will resume then."

Orias and Caim both bow their heads in the way I had missed from my wee human female.

Firn hurries out from behind the throne, moving toward Caim.

Glaine hesitates, staying by Sammael's side.

I meet the guard's green gaze.

He nods solemnly. "Yes, your grace. Right away."

As I expected.

I turn on Sammael. "My mage. Start conjuring. I require a length of charmed chains."

"My lord?" He glances around the throne room. It emptied quite quickly once I mentioned the chains, each of the other four turning to shadow and escaping through the cuts in the ceiling that, shadowless as I am, I've never used. "Where is the prisoner?"

My lips curve around my tusks, a mockery of an amused smile. "She is in the human realm," I tell my mage. "And we will both be going to retrieve her."

CHAPTER 4
HE'S BACK (AND HE BROUGHT A FRIEND)

SUSANNA

I grabbed my broom, but I also made another pitstop in my bedroom. Grabbing my Walkman, I popped my Bon Jovi cassette into the player, then slipped the headphones on over my ears. I used the clip to attach the player to the waistband of my leggings, tucking the headphones' wires under it so that they wouldn't get snagged on anything as I made my way back to the living room.

I've listened to this tape a hundred times. Practiced fingers worked the rewind button, followed by the fast forward when I went too far back, going until I cued up 'Runaway'.

Only once the familiar sounds of David Bryan's keyboard playing came in through the foam protectors did I grip the broom properly, ready to sweep up the salt circle and chalk sigil.

And I was about to. Really. But I've been a Bon Jovi fan from before they blew up with their 'Slippery When Wet' album, and despite Mindy's jab earlier, 'Runaway' is one of my fave songs. Jon Bon Jovi's vocals are killer on this track, and a lot of people don't know this, but Richie Sambora wasn't the lead guitarist for the band then. It was a studio musician who wailed on the guitar, making one rad song.

Is that why, instead of sweeping up the mess, I switch my hold on the broom and pretend it's a guitar in the privacy of my living room? Maybe, but that doesn't stop me.

I wish I'd gone to that concert with Mindy. I'd been psyched when she said Dan managed to score four tickets to the gig, especially since I've always had a thing for a guy with long, pale hair. Whether that's David Bowie, his tight-pants-wearing alter ego in *Labyrinth*, or Sebastian Bach, the lead singer of Skid Row, I jumped at the chance to go see him and Jon Bon Jovi on stage.

I looked forward to going… but then Dan mentioned that the fourth ticket was for Jeff. Jeff McNally is a classically handsome dude in his early thirties, with a perfect smile, short blond hair, and a way-too-preppy-for-me style. When he looks at me, he sees an innocent girl he can mold into a wife and mother, just like Mindy.

Barf.

I want love. *True* love. And maybe it hasn't happened for me yet. With the spell a big ol' bust, it might not. I mean, I dragged a… I don't know what he was, though I'm pretty sure I was right and he was a demon, so let's go with that… I dragged a demon through a portal because a magic spell said we were meant to be, only for him to *poof.* Disappear.

And, no, I'm not distracting myself with belting out the lyrics to 'Runaway' because I want to just forget that, after twelve years, I finally cast a spell in my grimoire for it to fail spectacularly.

I don't know why I'm so bummed. I'm used to rejection. My whole life, I've been compared to Mindy. My pretty, perfect sister, who I love dearly, don't get me wrong… but she's who everyone wanted me to be.

Jeff, especially.

Dan's co-worker has spent the last six months trying everything he could to get me to go out with him, and as soon as I knew Dan invited him to the concert, I asked Lissy if she wanted to grab a bite to eat with me after work that night so I could come up with an excuse to pass my ticket onto someone else.

Settle for Jeff McNally when I grew up on Judy Blume and Francine Pascal, and now that I'm in my late twenties, I still adore recent films like *The Princess Bride* and *Labyrinth* and *Legend*, each one with a male lead who will do anything for the woman they love?

No way.

See, I'm a romantic. If he were my true love, that strange dude with the glowing eyes and white hair—again with the long, pale hair—might be a little bit shocking to my human brain, but my human hearts says that we could make it work. There'd have to be a little step stool action so that I could reach his face, and as a virgin, I'd hate to think about how big his junk is if he's proportional… assuming he's got a dick under his tight pants because, unlike Jareth, I didn't notice a bulge there earlier. Then again, I was kind of taken aback by the whole tusks and horns and claw-thing he had going on. He might've had one that those dark pants of his hid. Pity I didn't get the chance to stare long enough to notice before he got one peek at me, probably thought I looked just as strange to him as he did to my eyes, then decided… true love? Nah.

Hey. It's okay. That's what I tell myself at any rate. Having to introduce that giant demon to Mindy as my new boyfriend? While her expression would've been worth grabbing my Polaroid camera to capture it, maybe it's for the best that my fantasy adventure started and ended with a spell gone wrong.

For now, I throw myself into enjoying the song through the guitar break near the end, dancing around the room in my sneakers. Once Jon starts up with the last couple of lines, I swivel, moving the broom, about to finally get down to some cleaning at last.

At least, that was the plan.

The whole two or three minutes I was playing around, pretending I was in the band, I kept the mess behind me. As I turn, I see the salt circle and the pentacle drawn in yellow chalk—and *two* demons.

This time, there's no denying that that's what I'm looking at. Definitely demons, and the one in the front is the giant from before. Hovering just behind him, as though it—*he*—is made of black smoke or spilled ink or, I don't know, *shadows* or something… there's a shape similar to the white-skinned demon, with matching horns and long, flowing hair that shifts softly though there isn't any breeze in my house. His eyes are glowing, too, even if they're purple instead of blue.

Oh, and he has a length of friggin' chains stretched out between his wavy black hands.

I sure as heck can't miss those; the chains, I mean, since his shadowy hands are somewhat hidden in the evening gloom in my living area. Gold and shining, they glow nearly as bright as the demons' unblinking stares.

The broom falls from my hand, clattering against the hardwood floor.

My heart beats like a drum, louder and faster than the rock music pumping through the headphones. I snatch them, yanking them off my ears.

"*She's a little runa*—"

The headphones off, I fumble with the wires, shoving it all away from me so that I can hear myself think. I shove so hard, the Walkman falls off of my waist. That hits the floor harder than the broom, and I can't keep from wincing. It cost almost two paychecks to buy the cassette player. I hope it didn't break—

Ah, jeez. *Break*, Su? You have *two* demons in your house now—and chains, can't forget the chains I'm back to gawking at—and you're worried about your Walkman?

I hold up my hands, warding them off. "Okay. Um. I don't know what's going on here, but I didn't read the spell again. Message received, you know? You don't want to be my true love, and… and…" Crud. "You have no idea what I'm saying, do you?"

Of course they don't. I'm not so arrogant as to believe that a demon from another world—if that's indeed where the portal leads—would know English just because it seems to be that case in every fantasy movie I've ever seen. If I had to spend twelve years working toward translating the grimoire… the same grimoire that brought these demons here… then that's gotta be the language they speak.

In fact, once the big, white demon starts rumbling something to the slightly less huge demon with the chains, I'd bet that he's speaking in the same language as the grimoire.

Like with the grimoire, I understand a word here or there. I'm certainly not fluent. I can read it better than I'll ever be able to translate it from the source, and that's with about six different language dictionaries in my hand.

So do I know what they're talking about?

Nope.

Do they have any idea what I was blathering about?

Uh-uh.

I gulp, grateful that I listened to Mr. Woodrow and drew that protective circle—

"Holy shit," I breathe out, stumbling back, my heel landing awkwardly on the Walkman. I kick the stupid thing aside as I make my quick retreat.

Because the blue-eyed giant? He just stepped over the circle of salt like it wasn't even there.

He glances over his shoulder, long white hair flowing kind of majestically as he turns to face the dark demon. The giant gestures for his buddy to follow him.

Only he *can't.*

As though there's an invisible wall in front of him, when the shadowy demon with the purple eyes tried to follow the white demon with the… hang on, is that a crown? I peer closer at him, focusing on the crystalline *crown* nestled between his black horns that I didn't notice before.

Who is he, I wonder.

A king?

Not a goblin king, not like Jareth, but a demon king?

Is that my true love? Am I—

What? Su. No. Focus!

I rip my gaze away from the king guy, looking at the other demon. He walked face-first into that invisible wall. I know he did. Now he's tracing the circle, using a single hand to test the border. My estimation of Mr. Woodrow goes up just a little bit when it becomes clear that it's the circle of salt keeping him in.

But why didn't it keep in the king? Because he's royal?

Because the magic knows he's my true love?

Because he's not a shadow like his pal?

I don't know, but his monstrous face assumes a very familiar expression. He kind of reminds me of Mindy when she gets annoyed with me over something. With a scowl, he points at the purple-eyed demon, points at me, then rattles off something that I can't make heads or tails of.

The other demon does.

He shoves his hands outside of the circle, every part of him that does going up in flames straight away. I shriek once I realize that that… that's happening alright. It's gotta hurt like heck, too, but the shadowy demon with the fiery hands—and the chains, can't forget the chains again—just makes a pushing gesture.

I don't know how he does it. More magic, I figure, but as he pulls his hands back inside of the circle, the fire goes out. They're back to being inky-black fingers, and maybe they're burned to a crisp beneath the hazy edge, but I can't tell.

Sorry, but I'm a little distracted by the fact that his hands are empty now. And mine?

They're clasped in a pair of glowing, golden cuffs latched on my wrists, the length of the chain stretched between them.

I yelp, shaking my hands, trying to get them off of me. They're warm. Not too hot that I'm burning the way the purple-eyed demon did, but it's toasty against my skin. And, you know, I'm trapped.

Trapped.

"What are you… no. Get these off of me. You can't do this!"

Turns out, the giant demon *can.*

While I'm screeching, flapping my hands ineffectively, he stalks right over to me. Next thing I know, he's picked me up easily, cradling me like I'm a friggin' baby.

He jerks his chin at the other demon. That crown must mean something because he doesn't hesitate. The shadowy demon does something else with his hands, and suddenly there's a wall of *fire* in front of him.

He hops through it.

The demon king marches toward it.

I shriek again. "No, no, no! I'm human, okay? I don't know what you two are, but I burn."

Nope. He still can't understand me. He does, however, pat my ass in what's probably supposed to be a soothing gesture, then ducks his head and walks right through the fire.

I screw my eyes shut, waiting for the sizzle as he burns me alive.

It doesn't happen.

Oh, thank God.

I sense movement, but there's a noticeable shift when he steps out of the portal again. The way my vision glowed red from behind my eyelids vanishes, and when I risk opening my eyes again, I'm in a hall that's slightly dark and gloomy. A handful of strange glowing lights are positioned every few feet on the stone wall. They alternate between blue and white, both shades powerful enough for me to see what's opposite of the wall.

Bars.

Gleaming silver bars.

Bars that lead to jail cells.

My heart leaps up to my throat. I nearly gag when the purple-eyed demon opens the nearest cell, stepping aside so that the king guy can carry me in.

Once he has, he eases me to my feet. I guess that's something. He could've tossed me to the cot in the corner or something, but instead of doing that, he waits until I'm standing on shaky legs before he snaps something at the other demon.

Instantly, he waves his hands, and the chains are gone.

A little too late, I think, considering I've gotten a better look at those lights. They're unlike any light-bulbs or fluorescents I've ever seen before, and the way they hover and twist, more of an orb than anything else, it looks like… magic.

Magic.

Well, I've always wanted to be like Alice. Take a tumble through a rabbithole and go on an adventure in another world… that was Suzy's dream. As Su, I was hoping for my own romantic hero.

And what did I get? A giant who is bearing down on me, his hand outstretched, palm up.

He pauses when there is about a foot separating us. I don't know his language, but I don't need to in order to get the gist. He wants me to put my much smaller human hand in his mitt.

I gulp.

The weird part… and I mean, the *really* weird part is… I kind of want to.

So I do.

A jolt passes between us, like an electrical shock times ten. My arm jerks. He doesn't let go of me, though. Instead, he folds his fingers over mine, tethering me to him.

And then he speaks, and if he wasn't holding onto me, I might've crumpled to the floor of the cell—

"I am Duke Haures. Lord of the Shadows. Ruler of the Flames," he rumbles, his English slightly accented, though there's no denying that, suddenly, *he's speaking English.* Which means I can't even pretend I don't understand it when his blue eyes blaze wildly and, in the deepest voice I've ever heard, he says:

"And you are mine, mortal."

CHAPTER 5
THREE DAYS

SUSANNA

He brought me to his world through a portal, said I was his *in English*, then tossed me into a dungeon.

How rude.

I did try to call after him, telling him it was a mistake. I mean, if I can understand him, then he can understand me, right? I don't know what happened, if his picking me up and carrying me through that fiery portal made it so that, once I was here… wherever *here* is… I could suddenly speak his demon language, but when I told him to wait, I heard English, but the sounds my mouth made were anything but.

Deciding I would deal with that later, I refused to let the big white demon walk away from me. The purple-eyed mage disappeared once he removed the chains and closed the door behind me, but at the sound of my voice, Haures—because I'll be darned if I call him *Duke*—hesitated just enough that I knew I had his attention.

He turned slowly. "Yes?" he grumbled.

So he wasn't happy. That made two of us.

I moved toward the bars, gripping one in each hand. "Okay. Look. My name is Susanna. I didn't mean to bother you or anything, and if it's fine with you, you can just send me back home through that portal thing. That would be rad. I'll be out of your hair—"

Haures lifted his hands, running his claws through his long, white hair, before saying pointedly, "You are not in my hair, mortal. You are exactly where I want you to be."

I squeezed the bars so tightly, my fingers ached. "Can't I just go home?"

He sniffed. "For now, you *are* home."

Only it's not my home. It's not *any* home. It's a dingy dungeon with chilly walls, a narrow cot, a single blanket folded up at the bottom, and—when I finally realized he'd gone away and wasn't coming back—a friggin' *hole* in the corner that has to be a toilet. It's weird, though. I put my hand over it, curious, surprised when there's just enough suction to suggest that it's like a vacuum. You do your business, and the hole takes care of it more efficiently than a flush.

That doesn't mean there isn't any running water

in here. On the other side of my cell, there's a… I guess the best way I can describe it is a tube. There's a top to it disappearing into the ceiling, a bottom that eats through the stone floor, but about a one-foot gap in between.

As curious as Alice, I thrust my hand between the gap. Only too late do I think that that might've been a stupid thing to do, but I sigh in relief when all that happens is that a steady flowing stream of warm water trickles over my fingers.

With water in one corner and a weirdo toilet in the other, this is clearly a place where someone could be abandoned for a long, long time. Without food, I could starve to death, but before I can even start to think that that's my fate, another demon appears outside of my cell.

For a second, I think it's the purple-eyed demon who—on Haures's orders—trapped me in here. That gets dashed to bits when the amorphous, black, shadowy shape with hazy horns and broad shoulders stalks down the hall, stopping right in front of my cell.

His eyes aren't purple. They're not blue, either.

This guy's are green—and that's not all. As I peer through the bars at him, the weirdest thing happens. In between one blink and the next, he goes from a mass of shadows to a nearly seven-foot-tall demon somewhat similar to Haures.

There are a few notable differences. This demon has deep-red skin, long black hair, and a long nose.

He's still huge, just not as massive as Haures, and he holds himself more rigidly than the duke. In my limited experience with both, Haures is all coiled-up tension, a dangerous demon masquerading as a crown-wearing duke. This demon? He screams 'soldier' at me.

Oh, and while Haures watched me earlier with a hint of heat and barely concealed interest that I'm pretty sure I'm not making up because I'm delusional, this guy? All I see is wariness and annoyance.

And food.

I take a step away, frowning. He didn't have a plate of food before when he appeared at the bottom of the stairs before marching down the hall toward me. Now? He has a crystal plate piled up with something that has to be charred meat. It looks—and smells—like barbecue, though that obvious fire scent might actually be coming from the demon instead.

I'm sorry. I should be grateful that they're not intending for me to starve, but…

"Where did that come from?" In case he doesn't know what I mean, I point. "The, um, plate."

The green-eyed demon glances at it. "I held the meat in my shadows to keep it warm."

In his *what*?

"Eat it," he orders. He crouches down, sliding the plate under a small gap between the bottom cell bar and the floor. He twists his wrist and, suddenly, he's holding a crystalline fork-type thing. He tosses it on the plate, and it must be made of stronger stuff because it doesn't shatter. "His grace will have my horns if he discovers that I was tasked to feed his mortal and you went hungry on my watch."

Oh, sorry. Don't want to get *you* in trouble…

I grab the plate, eyeing the meat closely. "What is it?"

"Ungez," is his answer, and I guess my newfound built-in translator goes beyond just communicating with the demons because I have a sudden mental image of what he means.

It's… I don't know. Made of the same shadows as the green-eyed demon was before he turned solid, with white eyes and the shape of a normal housecat on Earth, it has pointed ears, a pointed face, and a large, bushy tail that reminds me of an oversized squirrel.

Darn it, it's *cute*. Sure, this one is dead and cooked, but I… yeah. I'm no vegetarian, but I'm not hungry enough to gobble that down just yet.

I set it down on the edge of the cot. "I'll, uh, eat it later."

He jerks his chin, then turns away from my cell. He turns away, but he doesn't actually leave.

I take the chance to plead my case. "So… I'm not supposed to be in here. I think this is all one big mistake."

That demon I summoned is supposed to be my true love, not my *jailer*.

He shifts his bulk, looking over at me.

"There is no mistake. Duke Haures's first law says that humans are not allowed to learn of Sombra. Our realms are kept separate. Mortals and immortals"—*immortals*?—"do not mingle unless the gods will it." His green eyes darken. "How did a wee creature like you catch the duke's attention?"

Wouldn't he like to know…

At least I understand one thing. If I inadvertently broke one of the laws of this place, that would explain why the demon duke's first instinct was to put me in the dungeon. Plus, I learned something else, too.

"Sombra," I echo, purposely ignoring his question. "Is that where I am?"

In retrospect, it's kind of obvious. *Grimoire du Sombra*… it would make sense that the spellbook was talking about a place. True, I convinced myself that 'Sombra' was, like, a wizard or something and those were *his* spells, but maybe I wasn't all that far off…

"It is our realm," he confirms. "A refuge for demons and demonesses."

But not humans, I guess.

He turns to leave again, but pauses when I throw one more question at him.

"Hey. What's your name?"

He hesitates, as though not sure he wants to share it.

The demon just admitted what I suspected: he *is* a demon. I remember some of the books I read on demons and the occult while I was endlessly researching the spellbook. There are certain mythological and legendary creatures that, if you know their true name, you have power over them.

Hey. It's worth a shot.

When he finally grates out, "Glaine," I'm not so sure me having it will do anything since he did give it up at. Still, I try.

"Let me out of this cell, Glaine. Help me go home."

Not like I *want* to. For twelve years, I convinced myself that there had to be more than my mundane life. I finally have proof of it. If I were free to explore, or Haures really was my true love, ready to welcome me to his realm, I'd choose to stick around in a heartbeat.

But since I'm locked in a cell…

Glaine's eyes flash angrily. He bares his fangs at me and, for the first time since I arrived in Sombra a few hours ago, I'm just a little nervous.

He moves toward the cell, so close the tip of his long nose nearly reaches past the bars. "I am the head of Haures's guard. The duke has my loyalty. Do not ask again."

Okay, then.

I don't. The way he looks down at me so fearsomely, I know better than to test him.

Does that mean I keep my mouth shut?

I'm a younger sister. Of course not.

"How long does the demon duke guy plan on keeping me down here?"

My only answer is the slap of Glaine's solid feet against the stone hallway before he changes forms again, becoming shadow and vanishing up the stairs.

Darn it.

Glaine might not have had an answer for me, but neither do the other guards that come to tend to the human in the dungeon. Now, that might be because the head of Haures's soldiers tipped them off not to be too chummy with the human because I can't get a single word out of *any* of them. At one point, I thought the magic wore off and they couldn't understand me anymore, but whenever it's Glaine who comes down to patrol the empty dungeon, he'll at least talk to me, even if it's just to snap orders my way.

So, no, the other demons didn't know how long I'd be stuck down here—but on the third day, I finally get my answer when I wake up out of a slight doze, sit up on the cot, and find that Haures has been watching me sleep from his post out in the hall.

I don't know how long he was there. I don't have any idea what time it is. I lost all track of it, and only wish I'd remember to put my Swatch watch back on after I finished washing dishes the day I was nabbed by the demon duke.

That was only a nap, though, so I still consider it the third 'day'. I also don't know what took so long for Haures to check up on his human prisoner, but I'm not too keen on the way my heart jumps giddily to find him standing within arm's reach.

Darn it. I'd done everything I could over the last three days to pretend that I imagined that initial pull toward him, then the jolt when he touched my skin after having the purple-eyed demon remove the chains from me. I thought it worked—and then our eyes meet and I feel zapped awake.

Like our connection is electric in a world that doesn't have electricity, though it is *magic.*

So, it seems to me, is Haures.

There's something about him. You'd think that, after making me his prisoner, I'd never want to see his face again. If only.

I can't deny there's something pulling me toward him. The way he's staring at me now… I almost want to pinch myself to make sure I *am* awake.

It wouldn't be the first time I thought I saw him there in the gloom. Not even when I was conscious, either.

You see, I dream about him. And I know it's Haures because I don't change his features at all. It's like my subconscious has no problem with his monstrous appearance. And, really, is he that much of a monster; looks-wise, I mean? So he has horns. Claws. Tusks. Take them away and he could be any bodybuilder on Venice Beach, just without the golden tan.

Crud. I'm attracted to him. He locked me in a dungeon, and as though he's the villain that the ingenue heroine can't help but want, I have to fist my hand to keep from reaching through the bars to see if his skin is as warm as something tells me it must be.

I clear my throat. It's thick with something. Sleep, maybe, or an irrational lust that has me squeezing my thighs together as I stay seated on the cot…

"It's you," I say, pretending like I haven't spent the last three days hoping to see him for a third time. "Are you finally going to send me home again?"

A pang in my chest has me struggling to cover up my wince.

I ignore it.

Over the last three days, I've had plenty of pangs like that. There's this strange, unsettling feeling, deep in my chest, that seems to be connecting me to Haures. I don't understand it, and though I don't *not* like it, it's become annoying when there isn't a darn thing I can do about it.

I can go. I never got the chance to read the 'promise' part of the *verus amor* spell. I stopped at 'manifest', and it's pretty obvious that part worked. If I promised myself to him, I don't think I *could* leave Haures, but since I *didn't*…

We can chalk this up to a silly little girl playing around with forces she didn't understand, despite all the years of research and correspondence she had that made her believe otherwise.

Sound good?

To me, maybe, but not Haures.

At first, he shakes his head. So that's a no, I'm not going home. But then he crooks his finger, gesturing at his bulk with his claw.

"Come with me, mortal."

CHAPTER 6
DINE WITH ME

SUSANNA

I almost want to tell him to take a long walk off a short pier or something even more snotty.

Like, really?

Come with you, Haures?

Three days after he stole me from my house, leaving me down in the dungeon, claiming I broke some demon law that *I've* never heard of… three days of suffering with this *thing* in my chest, tugging me toward him, drawing me closer, wishing he'd throw me a bone and explain what the hell he meant when he said I was his… three days after he gave me every reason to stop believing in true love for the first time in my life, and *now* he wants to summon me this time, ordering me to go with him?

There are two reasons why I refrain from telling him to take a hike.

One? I want out of the cell. Period. Whatever he did to me so that I can understand the demons—because they're not speaking English, I'm just suddenly fluent in Sombran—it also makes it so that I can read their language. I found that out when I bugged one of the green-eyed guards patrolling the corridor outside of my cage, asking him if there was anything I could read since I was just so bored.

He did, almost begrudgingly, though I had to swallow a retort when he admitted that he received permission from the duke in order to do so. I was just happy to have any book at all, even that one. It was a history of the wars between Sombra and another demon plane known as Brille Rouge, and while it was a far cry from the romance books I devoured back home, at least it was something to distract me since my poor Walkman was abandoned back in Connecticut.

I needed something to take my mind off of my situation. It was one thing, being whisked away to a fantastical realm for the promise of a happily-ever-after. It's enough to be branded a criminal, tossed into a dungeon, and studiously ignored by the demon duke who I thought might actually be my true love.

He's not, clearly. I got fanciful ideas in my head, and now I'm paying for it.

I'm not the only one, either.

Mindy… does she know something happened to me yet? It's been three days, and I usually speak to her every other at least. When will she realize I've disappeared? If I don't show up at the call center, will they think of me as just another flaky employee, or will Lissy sound the alarm?

My book is out in the open. I never got the chance to clean up the protective circle. I feel bad for the Madison PD. Add the pentacle to the grimoire, and I wouldn't be surprised if Susanna Benoit isn't written off as another victim of Satanic Panic.

They'd be right, too, I think as I follow at Haures's heels, hurrying up the stairs so that his much larger stride doesn't leave me behind. I've been taken by a demon—a *real* demon—and he's made it clear that, whatever reason he had to Su-nap me, I'm not going back to Madison anytime soon.

And that leads me to the second reason why I gave in.

Curiosity.

They say it kills the cat, but I've been *dying* to learn more about the world he's brought me to. Not even because I'm itching to return home. I know heroines in stories like these are always eager to go back to the mundane human world. I guess I'm the opposite because, while I'm in Sombra, I want to drink it in.

That's the researcher in me. After owning the grimoire for nearly half my life, it's such a delight to discover that the *Sombra* mentioned in the title, *Grimoire du Sombra*, is a place. It's a world.

It's a fantasy.

So far, I know that Haures is its ruler, and that it had a ton of wars when a different demon wore the crown. The book I'm reading talks of a king—Yelios—and a queen—Alana—making it clear that Queen Alana was the ruler, and Yelios? He was her mate.

That one word caught my attention. Mate… The sudden ability to understand Sombran is a strange one. When I look at the pages, I see the unfamiliar language printed there, but it's like my brain provides the English translation instantly.

Mate… the moment I saw the word 'uxor', I instinctively understood that it referred to a mate. A bonded partner, with each demon only getting one.

It's their one true love.

I swear that I heard Haures refer to me as that before he disappeared through the portal the first time. Then again, maybe I'm just remembering how that was one of the formerly gibberish words that were in the *verus amor* spell. Either way, between the queer sensation in my chest and the way my body is reacting now that Haures is near, I have to wonder…

Is that what he meant by 'mine'? That I'm his mate?

If so, he doesn't tell me. Instead, after announcing that I will come with him, he stays quiet until we've climbed what has to be nearly four flights of stairs.

They took us out of the dungeon. At the top, Haures slides open a door made of stone, leading me out into a large room that's so different… so *striking*… I almost forget that I've spent three days peeing in an unusual hole in the ground.

It's beautiful, and like nothing I expect.

This must be where Haures spends most of his time. Not only because there are blue lights *everywhere*, all of them the same shade as his eyes, but the huge throne made of crystal, up on a raised dais, has got to belong to the demon duke.

The floor beneath my sneakers is slick and shiny. The tiles seem to mimic the crystal throne and his crystal crown, reflecting the orbs of light that illuminate the long, narrow room. Over my head, I notice that the ceiling has holes the size of a small pizza tray cut into it. Part of me wonders what would happen if it rains, while the other part is like a magpie, stunned by how sparkly everything is.

"This is my throne room," Haures says. "Where my subjects come to meet with their duke, and where I make the decisions that affect them all."

I get the sense that I'm supposed to be impressed.

I muster a small smile, doing my best to hide that, well, I *am*. "That's nice."

He grunts softly. "Come, mortal—"

"Susanna."

Haures glances over at me. "Did you speak?"

Sure did. "I said, my name is Susanna." He

doesn't get to call me Su. Not while he has a major stick up his butt. "And you're Haures. Right? Our introduction down in the dungeon happened so quickly, I thought I'd double-check."

"I am Duke Haures, Lord of the Shadows, Ruler of the Flames—"

"So I was right. Your name is Haures."

His brow furrows slightly. Huh. His ears are as pointed as any other demon I've seen, but unlike the others, his forehead is smooth. He doesn't have any ridges over his nose. Neither does he seem to ever shift to that wavering, shadowy shape like the others.

"Hey," I say, changing the subject because, as ever, I'm super friggin' curious. "This is your home—"

"Mavro is the capital of Sombra. This palace has been mine as long as I've worn this crown."

That's a lot of words for a simple 'yes'... "Cool. But I've seen a lot of those shadow demon guys milling around. Bodyguards, I guess. When they're not shadows, they've got this deep red skin. What about you?" I wave my hand at him. "You look like this now. What happens when you, you know, change?"

I thought it was an innocent enough of a question. Especially if I'm going to be stuck here, shouldn't he take it as a compliment that I'm interested in him and his people?

He scowls, and I gulp. I… I'm not scared. He

makes me nervous, and… and something I'm not ready to deal with just yet… but he doesn't scare me.

The scowl fades to a flat expression, as though I surprised him by not screaming again and trying to run away.

Why would I bother? With the spellbook left behind, it's not like *I* can really go anywhere else…

It takes him a moment to understand that I meant my question, and that I'll peer up at him curiously until he answers.

The scowl makes a triumphant return. "I don't change."

"Really? Why not?"

He clicks his claws together in obvious agitation. Even so, his deep voice is completely emotionless as he tells me, "Because I am the only Sombra demon currently in existence without his shadows. I am always as I am."

Right. Big and fearsome and too ruggedly beautiful for his own good…

"Wow. So that's why they made you the demon king?"

There goes his forehead scrunching again. Poor guy. He makes it too easy… "No. That is why I am the duke of Sombra. Now, come… Susanna."

Progress. "Where are we going?"

"Follow me and you shall see."

It takes a trip through two doors, then down a long hall before Haures leads us through another door into what has to be his dining room. As I gawk at my surroundings, he moves in front of me, blocking me with his giant demon body.

Haures rumbles in his chest as he peers down at me imperiously. "You will dine with me."

Wait… *that*'s why he pulled me out of the dungeon?

I smile at him sweetly. "I'd rather starve."

His eyes flash. "It wasn't a request. Take your seat."

I glance at the long, shiny black dining table stretching out behind him. It's different from what I'd expect from the duke. It's lavish. Polished. Way too dramatic after the icy way he rules over his throne room. His dining room is much more inviting, though I notice something interesting about the long table: it's set for two, with one chair at the head of the table, the other just to the right of it.

Oh. I'm not just supposed to 'dine with' Haures. He wants me at his side instead of watching me from the other end of the table. Almost like he wants me close… but since his actions so far have made it clear that—spell or no spell—there's no true love here, I don't understand it.

I blame it on my fuzzy brain. I've only eaten sparingly, ignoring most of the meals that the dungeon guards have slid into my cell these last three days. For one thing, I'm a little wary about *what* they're serving me. For another, anxiety does an awesome job of snatching my appetite away. I didn't even realize I *was* that hungry… until I take a breath and my stomach goes tight.

I can't identify any of what's laid out on the dinner table. Right now, it doesn't matter. The food, undeniably strange yet somehow tempting, smells like roasted spices and something vaguely floral. There's obviously meat—larger hunks of the roasted meat served to me in the dungeon—and something that could be a demon melon. Fruits, maybe, or sweet vegetables.

Swallowing back the saliva welling up in my mouth, I focus on the two chairs again. The one at the head of the table is obviously meant for the duke. It's a copy of the crystalline throne in his throne room, big and imposing, perfect for his massive bulk. The other one, though?

It's a smaller version, designed for either a tiny demon—or a human woman—in mind. It has a padded seat, too, and it's clearly not a chair meant for a dungeon dweller.

The reminder that that's where I've been all along with all of this luxury and brilliance and obvious displays of demon wealth and power only a few floors above me… it gets to me—and I let Haures know it.

I arch my eyebrow in a perfect mimicry of my

older sister. I even match her tone as I say, "I didn't think you'd eat with one of your prisoners."

Haures purses his lips around his tusks. "You are not my prisoner."

That's news to me. "I'm sorry. I guess I got the wrong idea with the chains and the dungeon."

Who is this Susanna? My whole life, I was the quiet one. The studious girl. I only ever got to be sassy when I was teasing Amy, the fun, young aunt. Mindy would sigh and tell me to grow up if I showed any hint of teenage rebellion and attitude, and after I found the *Grimoire du Sombra* and dedicated my twenties to translating it, I guess I did.

But, suddenly, it's like I can't help myself.

Then again, I grew up in a feminist-forward household. I kind of had to since Dad went out for milk one day when I was fourteen and never came back. Even before then, though, our mom led by example. She worked as a secretary while I was in school instead of staying at home, though she always told me that, if I chose to be a housewife when I got older, that was as valid a career as working for Mr. Walker at the ad agency was.

That was what Mindy wanted. Me? I just wanted a man who loved me for me, and I'm just not sure it can be this demon duke.

Especially when, instead of understanding my sarcastic quip, he says graciously, "You have nothing to be sorry for." And if that didn't make me sputter, following his comment up with, "A duchess does not apologize," does.

Really?

Well, it's a good thing I'm not a duchess, then.

Grabbing the tiny chair, he drags it out, waiting for me to take a seat.

I could say 'no'. I could refuse, but if I do, how much do you bet he'll just toss me back into the dungeon?

For some reason, Haures has decided to humor me tonight. Who knows? Maybe this is my chance. Either to convince him to let me go back home, since he obviously doesn't want me around, or to get a better understanding of why I can't help feeling drawn to the demon duke, even though I have every reason to hate him. Like two magnets, there's an undeniable pull between us. At least, to me, there is.

Haures? I can't tell, and the chance to get a better read on the big demon has me plopping down in the seat before I change my mind.

He nods in approval, the blue light winking off of his crystalline crown as he strides over to the head of the table, pulling out his own seat, and sinking royally into it.

I expect servants. He's, like, the not-king, right? He should have servants to cook this elaborate meal, then serve it.

Maybe he does. Maybe he gave them the night off so that they didn't have to deal with the stray human in the duke's castle. Whatever the reason, Haures grabs one plate, filling it with a little of everything before setting it down in front of me.

"Eat," he orders. "Then we'll talk."

I pick up the instrument that appears the closest to a fork. Made of crystal, like nearly everything else in here, it's the same three-pronged utensil that comes with the plates of meat the guards have been trying to feed me.

There are a few different familiar hunks on my plate. There's also a pale purple fruit that reminds me of a miniature plum, or a supersized grape. I spear it, then pause when I notice that the plate Haures made for me is the *only* plate he made.

"Aren't you going to eat?"

"I will after I've seen you fed, mortal."

I let that one slide because I'm a little bit suspicious when it comes to what he said before that. Oh, heck. I'm not, like, his poison-taster, am I?

Lifting the maybe-plum up so that I can get a better look at it, I frown. "Hey. You're not, like, gonna try to poison me, are you?"

Haures huffs, almost as if my tease—that's really not a tease, sorry—offended him. "If I wanted you eliminated, I'd send you to the shadows."

I don't know quite what that means, but… hey. Good to know. "So, I can eat this?" Because while I said I'd rather starve, I'm thinking twice now that my stomach is super unsettled. I just hope that it's hunger… and not something else. "It's safe for humans?"

"It should be."

My gaze slides over to the head of the table. "That doesn't really fill me with confidence, Haures."

I wait to see if he's going to correct me. To remind me that he's *Duke* Haures. I'll be happy to remind him that he's not *my* demon duke, and if he's going to insist on referring to me as 'mortal' instead of my name, I'll use his name instead of his title. But just like Mindy, he can sense when I'm gearing up for a fight, and he doesn't let me have it.

Instead, he admits, "You are the first human who has been in Sombra for as long as I have existed."

Something about the way he says that… "And how long is that?"

He leans back into his throne. "Far longer than your mere three decades, *Su*."

CHAPTER 7
THE ASHBALM FLOWER

SUSANNA

I blink.

Okay. I can forgive the nickname, even though I only want close friends and family to shorten my name. Otherwise I'm Susanna, and since the demon duke doesn't realize how awesome I'd be as a true love, he's never going to be one of them. But how does he have any idea how old I am?

It's rude enough that he aged me up to thirty. Still, it's a pretty close guess… and since his 'older' comment makes me think I might be dealing with a demon as old as Jesus Christ himself… like he truly is immortal, and as soon as I have that thought, something inside of me… that same *something*… tells me that I'm right. I'm looking at a pretty sexy Methuselah—

Wait. Sexy? What the heck, Su? Don't think that your demon jailer is sexy. Even if his sculpted cheekbones are sharp, his hair looks super soft, and his bare chest is tempting because he *never* wears a shirt, though I get it. With a body like his, he should show it off—

No.

Tusks, I remind myself. Horns.

Claws.

Giant.

It's the true love spell. It has to be. When Haures left me in the dungeon, I could stew over how messed-up that was. Definitely not how any guy should go about making a good first impression on his true love.

Over an elaborate dinner, sitting on this surprisingly soft chair, the light softening his harsh features… Haures is undeniably handsome for a demon. I don't look past his monstrous features. I actually embrace them because he's not just some regular dude.

Though he is a demon *duke*, and while he doesn't seem like the kind of guy to try a nickname on for size, the confident way he called out my age and my chosen nickname while being careful not to answer anything about himself… oh, boy. I'm in trouble.

Just as I have that thought, two very weird things happen.

First? That strange sensation in my chest, kind of like a thin wire inside of me that reaches out, connected to someone else… connected to *Haures*…

gives a sharp tug. I gasp, rubbing my breastbone with the heel of my hand, but that doesn't help. If anything, it *thrums*, pulling me toward the demon duke at the same time as a sudden certainty hits me.

It tells me that I'm not imagining things, this demon *is* my true love, and that he has a sudden desire to sweep the mounds and mounds of food onto the floor so that he can use his claws to shred off my clothes and bury his face into my cunt to see if I taste as good as I smell.

Whoa.

So, yeah. That definitely didn't come from me. And if it didn't come from me…

My lips part, heat flooding my face as I peer over in surprise at Haures's suddenly impassive expression.

That was the first thing.

The second?

His expression is unreadable, but Haures's brilliant blue eyes flare, going so bright, they're almost as white as the rest of him as he darts out his tongue, toying with the tip of one of his tusks as his hand… instead of shoving the food away, he drops his hand to his lap.

I shift in my chair before he has any clue what I'm about to do. Rising up just enough that I can peek over, his fingers are curled around the very, *very* obvious bulge that his pants do nothing to hide.

Not for the first time, I'm reminded of *Labyrinth*. Marketed as a family-friendly film, I was in my mid-twenties when it came out, and, while it's quickly become one of my favorite movies, let's just say that David Bowie's bulge should've gotten its own listing in the credits.

Holy shit. The demon duke puts the goblin king to shame.

He clears his throat.

My cheeks blazing now, I slip back into my seat and set down my fork.

"Well," I begin, my voice sounding a little shaky with embarrassment for having been caught peeking at him under the table. "I'm here. The only human… but I've got a question. *Why* am I here?"

I mean 'in Sombra'. Haures interprets my question a little differently.

"I was not expecting to be summoned. I was in a meeting when you called for me." A frown, and then, "I am often meeting with my people. There have been many villagers coming to the capital to talk with me this cycle. I couldn't risk them knowing you are here. In your cell, I knew where you were and that you were safe."

Oh. How nice.

Instead of putting me up in, like, a guest room inside of this massive palace-type place he's living in, Haures's genius plan was to take the human woman and lock her up without anything other than the possessive way he growled at me before disappearing for days.

You are mine…

It was Glaine, one of the green-eyed soldiers that explained I was in breach of the duke's first law, and that's why I was tossed in the dungeon to pee in a hole. And maybe that's what *he* thought, but that feeling in my chest… it's telling me that Haures means what he says.

He was hiding me to keep me safe, all because I'm a human.

His human.

"So I'm not a prisoner. Just a dirty, little secret." Well, *that*'s nice, too. "I guess you don't want to anyone to know that you let a human in on your watch. Who knows? They might turn on you."

It was more a grumpy tease than anything, but the way Haures places his elbows on the top of the table, steepling his claws… I get the feeling that I was way closer to the truth than I ever could've imagined.

Especially when he nods gravely. "There are those in Sombra that would take the opportunity to test my hold on the crown if they thought they could snatch it from me."

I snort. Sorry, but I can't help it. "Good luck."

He cocks his head.

"What? You're the biggest demon I've seen so far. And," I add, waving my hand at him, "you definitely stand out. You just ooze power. They'd have to be morons to challenge you."

His expression turns thoughtful. "And, yet, you

have no trouble doing so. A mere mortal who's been thrust into a new world. You have no fear of me."

I don't like the way he said that. "Should I?"

"No."

It's a simple response.

No.

Phew.

Haures lowers his hands to the table, leaning back into his seat again. "As you can obviously see for yourself, I am unlike most Sombra demons, Susanna." Huh. Back to Susanna again… almost as though he can read me the same way I can him, and he only used my nickname earlier to *prove* that. "I told you before, but it's because I'm a shadow demon born without any of his own. My essence is… different from my people. But my bonds are stronger because of it… and there is no denying that you and I, we share a bond."

Well, when the demon duke puts it as bluntly as that, giving a name to that strange feeling inside of my chest… bond. Yeah. Duh, Su. Wasn't that how that book described the relationship between Queen Alana and King Yelios? That they were *bonded* mates?

I called Haures my true love because that's what the *verus amor* spell promised to bring me if I read the manifestation spell. But… is he my *mate*?

Is that why he becomes even more attractive to me, the longer I sit here? Why I dreamed of him, and why I would've gone searching for him if those bars hadn't kept me trapped? Not because I wanted to tell him off, but because I'm drawn to him in a way I've never been drawn to any other guy before?

Is that why I've always equated cracking the *Grimoire du Sombra* with my own happily-ever-after?

I need to hear him say it. "What does that mean? Am I… are you… are we true loves?"

He doesn't answer me right away. Large and imposing and smelling of smoke and a spicy musk that calls to me over the lure of the food… Haures stares at me unblinkingly for a moment before he finally admits, "The gods say that we are."

Okay. Bringing religion into it. Not what I expected from a demon, but okay.

I bite down on the corner of my mouth. I still have the image in my head of me being sprawled out on the table, Haures feasting on me instead of the meal. If that's what comes along with being a true love… we can work our way up to that bulge, but for now—

Hang on.

The *gods* say.

"What do *you* say?"

He pauses for a moment, thinking over it, then rumbles, "There is a flower that grows in the darkest shadows at the edge of Sombra. The ashbalm flower. This is a realm of fire. Of ash. But with that comes the dark. If one braves the shadows and retrieves the ashbalm, it can snap any bond in the hands of a bondmaster." He pauses for another moment before dropping the bomb: "I told you I was unlike the other Sombra demons. I have no shadows of my own, but I know we have a bond because I *am* a bondmaster."

I blink. Is he saying what I *think* he's saying…

He's a bondmaster. He can sense our bond, but with this ashbalm flower thing, he can get rid of it, easy as that.

He can erase the fact that we're true loves with, like, the snap of his fingers.

Claws.

Whatever.

"And you're going to go get?"

His lips twitch just enough to match the fleeting flash of amusement skittering down what is our very obvious bond.

"No, mortal. *You* are."

If I wanted you eliminated, I'd send you to the shadows…

That's what he said. Don't think I haven't forgotten. So, either I'm dead, or I lose my true love. Depending on how generous my demon duke is, I could be booted back to Connecticut, my adventure over, or tossed into the dungeon again because, then, I really would be breaking the first law.

It's a lose-lose for me either way.

Wonderful.

But what else can I do?

I WISH I HAD A FLASHLIGHT.

To be honest, I'm wishing a lot of things at the moment, but that one is at the top of my list.

Haures wasn't whistlin' Dixie when he said that his demon realm was made of fire and ash and shadows. After he sat there, watching me eat enough food under slight protest that he considered his pet human —for now—he brought me to the throne room again. As though this was all planned, the purple-eyed demon who put me in chains was waiting by the throne.

His name is Sammael, and I now know that he is Haures's personal mage. I'd thought that what he did was magic, and I was right. He can cast spells of his own, and that includes something Haures called a travel spell.

In Sombra, demons that can change from their solid red-skinned form to misty shadows travel quicker than on foot. As a human, it would take days to get from the capital where Haures keeps his palace to the edge of shadows where I'm supposed to find and pluck and bring this ashbalm flower back to him. But if you have a mage to open a portal within the realm, taking you from point A to point B in the blink of an eye, the trip is done in no time.

Accepting I really had no choice, I followed Sammael through it, coughing when I landed outside somewhere.

It's hot. Like, middle of August, heatwave in

Connecticut *hot.* The shift in weather was so gnarly, my ponytail almost instantly started to droop. It's gotta be hotter than ninety out here, with air that stinks of rotten eggs. My lungs burned with every breath I took. The ash under my feet gave way with each step, and I entertained running into the red-tinged night when the alternative was willingly entering a patch of shadows so dark, it was like midnight out in the woods, no matter what time of day it was.

Hell, I decided when I noticed bursts of fire in the distance, a pair of moons shining weakly overhead, and more than a few bleached-white skulls buried in the ash outside of the shadows. Haures lives in a crystal palace, but this world?

It's Hell.

Makes sense. He is a demon, after all. Lord of this realm, and the guy who thought it was a great idea to send me into a dark forest with only the advice that I would know when I was growing closer to the ashbalm flower when I scent it.

Right. Like I had any idea what *that* means…

Sammael couldn't come with me. Haures said that this quest was mine and mine alone, and that meant the mage was to wait outside of the shadows until I returned, needing to hitch a ride back to the palace—with or without the ashbalm flower.

Remembering how rejected I felt when he mentioned how easy it would be to snap this growing bond between us, my stubborn side decided I *would* return with it or die trying.

Of course, I thought that before I took a deep breath—coughing again when it seemed like my insides were scorched—then pumped myself up right before I entered the shadows. On the plus side, it's a good ten, fifteen degrees cooler in there.

On the downside, I can barely see in front of my face.

A flashlight would come in handy. What makes it worse is that, the farther I go, wandering aimlessly, the more tiny white pinpricks that appear about a foot or two above the ash.

I'm ashamed to admit it took me way longer than it should've to recognize that they were *eyes*.

Because I'm not alone in here. Nope. And though Sammael warned me not to go too far off the path because that's where I should find the ashbalm flower, that's easy for him to say. First of all, I can't see a path. Second? When it finally does hit me that there are some critters in here, watching my every move? I start to go in any direction where there aren't that many eyes.

And third?

Shortly after I entered the shadows, my leg warmer got snagged on something sharp. Not thinking clearly, I bent down, grabbing it, shrieking when I lifted it in front of my face.

It was a *bone*.

Yeah, I almost high-tailed it right out of there. Only remembering how I've never stayed where I wasn't wanted had me shuddering, then tossing the bone as far from me as I could before carrying on.

Without a flashlight, I just bumbled around blindly. It's a small relief when my eyes adjust to the darkness enough that I can kind of see what's around me, thanks to the slight glow from the red-tinged moon and slightly gold sliver hanging next to it in the pitch-black sky over my head. I say 'small relief', though, because once I *do* see, it's easy to tell that the white eyes are attached to fuzzy shadow creatures that could be friendly, or could be deciding which part of me would be the juiciest.

I don't panic. If I wasn't stinging so badly from Haures's rejection, I might have, but I'm determined to do this. Follow my nose. That's what he implied. I would know I was near the ashbalm flower when I could smell it.

All I can smell is that same rotten egg stink—until, suddenly, the scent of garlic and sauce, baked dough, and savory pepperoni fills my nostrils.

Pizza.

I smell *pizza.*

Now, I've only been in Sombra for, like, three days. One thing I can say for sure? Dominos might be all over the US, but I don't think they've managed to branch out into demon realms just yet.

But that's pizza, and though I did eat enough

during my meal with Haures, nothing in this world or any other will ever be able to come between Susanna Benoit and a slice of pepperoni pizza.

I jog in that direction, sniffing every few seconds to make sure I haven't lost it. Just like with Haures, it's a compulsion. Like I *need* to find the source of the delicious aroma, and when I do, I'm not sure if I should be pleased at what I stumble upon… or disappointed that it's not pizza.

Because it isn't.

It is, however, the most interesting flower I've ever seen.

About eight inches tall, including the black stem, its petals are made of flame. They hover on top of the dark pistol, at least a half-inch above the flower itself, wafting gently though there sure as heck isn't any breeze in here.

The ashbalm flower. It has to be.

Remembering Haures's final instructions, I know to be careful in plucking it from the ash. The stem itself isn't just black shadow. Like the ground it's sprouted from, it's also ash, and if I'm too rough with it, it'll crumble into nothingness.

And if the flames that make up the petal go out? The flower is worthless.

Careful, Su. Crouching low, I dig my fingers into the ash, trying to find the base of the ashbalm flower's stem. Once I think I've found it, I take a deep, steadying breath, then yank with just enough pressure to pull it out of the ground.

The flames waver, but they don't go out.

Phew.

Slowly, I tell myself. Slowly, I rise, holding the stem gently. Some of the ash falls away. I freeze, but I guess the flower is sturdier than I first imagined because it's still shining brightly.

There. I have it. And once I bring it back to Haures, everything should go back to normal…

Look at me. I didn't have to traverse a maze like Sarah, hoping to find my baby brother at the center. Instead, I braved these supposedly deadly shadows to retrieve a flower and, darn it, I *did*.

I got my heroine moment after all, even if I won't get my happy ending—

A deafening roar rents through the darkness, so loud that I squeak, dropping down, only just managing to keep from losing the flower at the same time.

My ears echo, but it's not just the aftermath of the roar.

It's an *answering* cry. A warrior's cry.

A *demon's* cry.

I knew I wasn't alone in here, but now I have proof that it's not just those strange shadowy critters following me. There's someone *else* in the shadows, and they're in trouble.

I don't even think about it. Standing up again, I

give myself two seconds to make sure the ashbalm flower is okay. When I see the flame is still flickering, bright as ever, though it miraculously doesn't burn me where it fell against the top of my hand, I adjust my hold on it.

I cradle the flower in my cupped palms, and then I run.

CHAPTER 8
SHADOWS

SUSANNA

Bear.

That's the only word I can think of to describe the shadow creature that's battling against a Sombra demon male I've never seen before. Mainly because his red eyes burn through the darkness as he lets out another warrior cry, echoing the one that had me running toward the sound.

Now, should I have run *toward* the sound? Probably not. But if there's one thing that both Mom and Mindy imparted to me growing up, it's not to be just another bystander. That's how kids keep going missing. If you can help, do so.

Of course, they never expected that I'd find myself stumbling upon a battle between a creature that manages to dwarf one of the seven-foot-tall demons who live in this fiery world, but the idea is the same. Despite being a ferocious demon himself, that raging grizzly bear-type shadow beast is bearing down on him with all the fury of a bear back on Earth.

Immortal, I remember. That's what Glaine said. Sombra demons are immortal, but tell that to the monster who looks like he won't stop until he rips the other demon from shadowy limb to shadowy limb.

These woods are dark. Like, totally dark. Even so, there is something about watching the shadow creature and the demon dude move that helps me pick them out among the other shadows. Almost as though they're just one shade lighter than the pitch-black woods so, if I squint, I can find them even if they're quiet.

But they're not quiet, are they?

The beast roars. The demon howls in answer, trying to get the beast to back off, but I guess it doesn't work because, right as I cradle the ashbalm flower to my chest, tiptoeing closer so I can see what's going on without making myself a second target, the shadow bear with glowing white eyes the size of baseballs rears back its arm, then swings with so much might, it slams into the demon, knocking him to the ash.

It's friggin' quick, too. Before the demon can get up and protect himself again, the shadow bear-monster-*thing* lumbers toward him, pinning the demon with a paw the size of a serving platter.

The demon bucks. He can't get up. The hit

must've knocked the wind out of him, leaving him on his back as the bear gets ready to swipe at him again.

No.

Cupping the ashbalm flower with my left hand, I reach down with my right. Digging in the ash desperately, I search until I find another bone fragment. I try not to think about how easy it was to find a length of bone like that in here—though if bears battle demons, that might explain it—and just jump up, making as fierce of a sound as I can.

Okay. I kind of sound like George of the Jungle, that cartoon I used to watch growing up in the late 60s. Or maybe Tarzan. I don't know. I don't really do much to frighten the bear, and when I throw the bone at it, I think I just made it angrier.

Great. So now that it'll slaughter the demon *and* me.

No. I can't let that happen.

Think, Su.

Think.

Wait—

Fire.

He's a shadow creature who lives in the dark. And while there's plenty of ash in here, the ashbalm flower is the only fire I've seen in the shadows. The bear's eyes are also much wider than the other shadow beasties. What if… what if he's not fond of fire?

Only one way to find out.

It stinks that I'll probably end up sacrificing my

flower to save the demon, but… hey. It's not like I really wanted to break this bond with Haures anyway. And if I can save a life, it's worth it.

Hoping like heck that it'll work, I grab the ashy stem with my thumb and pointer finger on my right hand. I daringly take three quick steps closer, still keeping enough distance that I'll at least have a heads up to my imminent demise if the bear thing targets me next.

Oh, Su. You didn't really think this through, did you?

Ah, well. Here we go.

Hoping that I won't just blow out the flickering flame, I start wafting it, moving my arm quickly, feeding it some oxygen. If I can breathe here—even if it's so hot, that's a struggle—then there's oxygen, and when you use oxygen to feed a fire, it grows.

Just like this one does.

Within seconds, the petals become a fireball. The bear is mesmerized by it, so captivated, it momentarily forgets the demon under its grip. As I shout again, I see him wiggle himself out as the monster loses its focus.

He's still too close. If the creature decides to ignore the fire and go for the demon again, it'll be able to do so easily.

So, knowing that I'm probably kissing this flower goodbye, I use the element of surprise to dash forward with the flames, then fling the fireball at the shadowy bear.

The fire hits it in the chest area. I don't know if it hurts so much as surprises the beast, but it falls back on its rump before hurriedly righting itself on all fours, lumbering off into the woods.

I turn toward the demon in time to see him gingerly climbing to his feet. He twists his head to the side, cracking his neck. He shakes out both arms. He tests his weight, and once he pronounces himself whole, he peers at me with blazing red eyes.

I swallow roughly. "Hey," I ask in Sombran, my voice thrumming with the unfamiliar language. "You alright?"

His gaze takes me in, top to bottom. And then, in a gravely voice, he says, "Who are you?"

Not a thank you, but what did I really expect? To this demon, I'm probably as much of a monster as that—

Arkoda.

I shake my head. I don't know where that word came from. The magic seems to have made it so that I understand Sombran, but it's like I know even more than that. Through this bond between Haures and me, I'm kind of able to pick up on things that the duke would know.

Like how the grizzly bear-looking shadow demon is a fierce predator—and known demon-killer—called the arkoda.

And red eyes on a demon male? This guy is a hunter who would've been in the shadows to find small prey beasts to hunt and cook for dinner, like the ungez Haures's cooks kept trying to feed me during my stay in the dungeon.

But while I know more about Sombra, this demon is acting like he's never seen anyone like me before—which he wouldn't have, would he?

Who are you?

I know it's not what he means, but I try anyway. "Um. I'm Susanna."

"You are… you're not a Sombra demon."

What was his first clue? "I'm not."

He continues to peer at me, his eyes a pair of stop lights as he frowns.

"Why are your ears round? And your teeth… they are small and flat. How can you eat meat?" He snorts. "Your eyes are dead. You have no light, or horns to protect your brow. Is that how your sort of feeble demoness exists? Or have the shadows overtaken you already the way I've heard that they can?"

How nice. I save a demon, and how does he repay me? He insults me. No 'thanks', not even a flippant 'I could've handled that', but nitpicking my very normal human features?

I should just cut my losses and go. I saved him, so I did my good deed for the day and can move on with a clear conscience. There's no reason to entertain this… but that doesn't stop me.

Now, do I expect him to know that I'm a human? Not really. Haures said I was the only one in his lifetime, and the way this red-eyed demon seems appalled by my appearance, we can't have been common even before Haures was in charge.

Still.

Tilting my head back so that I can meet his confused stare, I start by saying, "I'm not a demoness—"

"She is human." The male voice explodes around us like thunder, crackling like lightning. "At long last."

I spin around. Crouching into a defensive stance as though he didn't just get his butt kicked by that arkoda, the demon backs up against me like he's determined to protect me.

That might've been his next mistake. It made him a target when, if he'd just taken off into the shadows like that beast did, I would've been the only one left to face…

No one.

"Who are you?" I pause, then swivel, searching for who could've said that. I've gotten so much better, seeing in the shadows, and there's the demon I saved from that bear thing—that *arkoda*—and too many tiny white pinpricks belonging to other teeny tiny shadow creatures that remind me of goblins… no, *gremlins*… but a man with a voice that sounds like Darth Vader should be easy to find.

He's not.

"Where are you?" I demand instead.

"I am Yelios. King of Sombra. And I am everywhere, dear mortal."

Ignoring how impossible it is for him to be *everywhere*—or how slimy it feels to have him call me a 'dear mortal'—I focus on something else that stands out to me.

King? But I thought… "Haures is the duke—"

His laugh develops a cruel, sardonic edge. "A shadowless spawn who has stolen my crown. I do not care about that. All I want now is my mate."

A shiver runs down my spine.

No. I… I read about him; if he's the same king as the one in my book, that is. King Yelios, and his mate. Queen Alana. A bonded pair from ages ago who ruled Sombra together during the time of the wars between this realm and one of the neighboring demon worlds.

But she died. Like, forever ago, she died in one of the campaigns. And because not even death can sever a bond—even if the ashbalm flower is supposed to—Yelios followed her into…

Crud.

The shadows.

He followed her into the shadows, hoping to be with his queen together in the Sombran version of an afterlife.

Well, if I can believe that this disembodied voice is who he says he is, then it looks like he hid out in the woods after his queen perished. Fine. Good. He can stay here because, like he pointed out, I'm just a human. I can't help him with his long dead mate, right?

I don't know where he is, so, with as subtle a gesture to the other demon to follow me as I can make, I start to edge away from the clearing we're in.

I make it about five steps before I slam up against an invisible wall that reminds me of the one that kept Sammael trapped inside of the protective circle in my living room.

My nose smarts. So do my knees. It was the same as walking face-first into a solid glass door with no give to it at all.

I stumble back.

"There," he purrs, "now you understand that we will have this conversation, human, whether you want to make a deal with a demon or not."

Most decidedly, the answer is *not*. "Why me?" I ask.

"Because you belong to the usurper. I can sense the bond tying you together. He was a fool to let you wander in my realm, little mortal."

Usurper… Haures?

"I was looking for something—"

"Yes, and I was waiting for you."

Whether the demon tried to follow me before I got my face smashed, I don't know, but he's suddenly in front of me, bowing his shoulders, making himself seem even more imposing as he shouts up into the dark.

"I will protect her. You shall not threaten the human!"

Sweet. Useless, I think, but sweet.

Yelios doesn't think so.

His voice booming around the shadows, he snaps, "Silence, Dagon."

The air shifts. I wouldn't say it was wind so much as a whipping gale that has me cowering in the face of it. Only I'm not what it's after. That's the demon—*Dagon*—who is once again knocked off of his feet by the force of it.

As I watch in horror, the wind becomes a patch of impossibly black shadow that covers every inch of him except for his eyes. With his mouth hidden, he can't even scream, though I bet he's ripping his throat raw with his muffled hunter cries. He struggles against the shadows undulating over him. There's no doubt in my mind that they're pinning him down more effectively than the arkoda did.

Or that Yelios is responsible for it.

"Let him up," I holler. "Let him go!"

"Your soft heart will be your undoing, human. You want me to show him mercy? Spare his life so that I don't use his essence to feed my shadows? Tell me… what will you give me in exchange if I do what you say and let Dagon go?"

Because I *am* a soft touch at heart, the answer

'anything' is on the tip of my tongue… until it hits me that, for the second time, he used the demon's name.

"Wait— you know him? The hunter?"

Was this all some kind of trap? Something these two set up to snare the unsuspecting human woman? The fierce way Dagon's eyes are flashing say otherwise, but how the heck am I supposed to be sure?

"I know all," the voice says smugly. "More than even the doppelseers do. They see, but I *know*, and I know that you, human, are the key to everything I've spent ages waiting for."

Uh. That doesn't sound so great. Bogus, really. Having some eldritch horror tell me that he's been waiting for *me*…

Yeah. I don't think Haures is involved, and I doubt Dagon is, but this was totally a trap.

"What do you want from me?" I ask.

"Your firstborn child."

Is he serious?

"Okay, Rumplestiltskin."

"I am not *Rumplestiltskin*," he answers, managing to name the fairytale character perfectly even in his Sombran accent. "I am Yelios, King of Sombra, and that is my demand. Vow you'll give me your firstborn spawn, and I will spare the hunter."

My initial reaction is to tell him no. I've never thought seriously about kids since, you know, *virgin*, but the idea of sacrificing my firstborn for some dude I just met… uh-uh.

Then I think about it. Really think about it.

What am I really sacrificing?

Haures and I won't have a bond once I find another one of those ashbalm flowers and release him from it; even if I don't want to, it's clear to me he does, and I won't saddle someone with me who doesn't want me. No bond means we definitely won't have any kids here, and if I return to Earth and settle for some human guy to make Mindy happy, I'm not worried. The duke's first law says that there's no contact between our worlds. How can a spirit haunting the dark woods manage to have any claim to a baby in Connecticut?

He might not be Rumplestiltskin. I'm still going to treat Yelios like that, running through any obvious loophole in my mind. When I can't find any reason to let the shadows suffocate Dagon, I take a deep breath and say, "Deal."

"Vow it, human. Give me your promise."

Yeesh. These Sombrans and their promises. "Okay. Fine. I vow it."

That must've done something because, with another thunderous clap, the shadows disperse. Dagon chokes, but he's alive, and I only hope that my promise was enough to get Yelios off my back so that I can finish the search for the ashbalm flower and get the heck out of here.

And then the former king says, "It is done. When you give birth to the usurper's spawn, it is mine. Until then, I will take one thing that you hold dear in exchange. When I get what I want, you get it back."

There is no deal for that one. Yelios makes his pronouncement, and before I can realize how I've been maneuvered into *that* agreement, the air shifts. It turns lighter, and I didn't even realize how the weight of my surroundings was pushing me down until he's gone.

Because he's gone, and I'm left to wonder what the heck I just agreed to.

I STILL DON'T HAVE AN ASHBALM FLOWER.

Just because I don't want to sever this bond doesn't mean that I'm about to walk into Haures's castle empty-handed. I'm stubborn that way. I want to rub it in his face that I found the flower *and* beat that arkoda monster.

Only one problem: I can't find it. Can't smell it, either.

I try. Even though the idea that Yelios is lurking nearby has shivers running up and down my spine, I try, but it's pointless. It's like there was only one of those flowers in these dark woods, and I lost it—

"Human?"

My shoulders hunch in annoyance.

Right. Make that two problems.

As if insulting me earlier wasn't bad enough, after

the *second* time I saved him from the shadows, Dagon decided he wanted to become *my* shadow. Without a word, he simply started to follow after me. Figuring it wasn't worth an argument, I let him.

But calling me 'human'?

"Yes?" I ask through gritted teeth.

"Why did you save me?"

"Why are you following me?" I retort.

"Because you saved me," is Dagon's answer. "Why did you, female?"

I sigh before telling him again, "Susanna."

He pauses, frowning.

I resist the urge to roll my eyes. Aren't these demons used to common decency and using someone's name instead of what they are? I don't call Haures my 'demon duke', even if that's how I think of him, but 'human' and 'female'... "My name is Susanna."

"And I am Dagon of Caol. Fierce hunter," he says before fisting his hand, then beating himself in his shadowy chest. "And I pledge myself to your service."

Huh?

"Um. That's okay."

He firms his jaw. "I insist. Tell me what you require, and I will do it."

Oh, boy.

You know what?

Fine.

"Did you see that flower I had before the flame

went out? It's the ashbalm flower. It grows in these shadows, and I need to find another one."

"Very well. Then I will endeavor to help you find the flower."

I give him a thin-lipped smile and decide, hey, maybe he knows enough about the forest that he can help. As long as we avoid any more of those arkodas, we should be good.

And I keep up that silly hope for nearly another hour before I finally call it and ask Dagon if he can help me find my way back to Sammael.

He does, and though Sammael seems visibly stunned that I returned with another demon instead of the flower, he says nothing as he prepares a portal back to the capital.

CHAPTER 9
DAGON

HAURES

When Sammael's portal opens in my throne room, I hold my breath.

The bond still exists. I knew it would. It had to. Between my power and that of the essence of the ashbalm, I could snap it easily. I would need the flower brought back from the shadows on the edge of Sombra to do so, and it's the flickering flame hovering over the edge of the flower made of ash that I'm searching for as figures begin to materialize in the throne room.

I have to let her choose. To tether a human female to me for eternity… I am ruthless. I am fierce. I am Lord Haures.

But I am not cruel, and to keep such a treasure as my Susanna without giving her the chance to be free of me… I couldn't do it. It wouldn't be fair. I need her to accept me fully, and that includes choosing to keep our bond even if I offer her the opportunity to sever it.

I did. I sent her off to the shadows, knowing that it was a calculated risk I had to take. She was given enough of a clue to find the ashbalm flower. Staying close to the edges, she shouldn't be in any danger.

There was a moment while she was gone when I experienced a nervous quiver coming from Susanna's side of our bond to mine. Almost as if she was frightened, but it was there and gone a moment later. She closed me off, but that fleeting instant changed me.

She *is* my mate. Whether she returns with the ashbalm flower or not, it doesn't matter. I will do anything I can to convince Savannah that the gods gave her to me for a reason, and if she truly wants to leave me behind, she can wait another cycle until the next ashbalm flower blooms in the shadows.

So I hold my breath, and I wait, and, gods damn it, I *hope*.

Susanna stumbles through the portal first. I shift in my throne, every instinct in me warring against the need to project strength. Indifference. If a single one of my people knew just how easily this wee slip of a mortal could bring me to ruin, not even charmed chains and solid bars would keep her safe from my enemies.

There haven't been any wars in Sombra since I

took the crystal crown. My subjects both fear me *and* revere me, but I have no illusions. There are plenty who, given the chance, would cackle gleefully to see me toppled from my seat of power in Mavro.

Susanna could do it. And for the promise of her essence, I'd let her…

Following right behind Susanna, I see a demon in his solid form. When Sammael left with Susanna, he'd changed to his shadows. I assumed he changed back—and then the demon jerks upright, eyes searching the room, a predator's gaze…

A predator's gaze with *red* eyes.

A hunter.

Sammael steps into the throne room last, taking the portal with him. As before, he's in shadows, purple eyes blazing out of the dark depths, but he changes back quickly.

There are times I can't deny a hint of jealousy that my subjects can switch between forms so easily while I'm stuck as I am. I hide it, of course, but at the moment? It doesn't bother me.

Not when there's another male in the throne room, taking his place near my mate.

I find Susanna's hesitant expression. Her hair—the only part of her that is reminiscent of shadows—is falling to the side, curling around her slender shoulder. Ash is dashed across her cheek, another streak along her little white hands.

Her empty hands.

My heart jolts to see that she's returned without the ashbalm flower, while the rest of me burns to know why this hunter thinks he can stake any sort of claim to my Susanna.

"You brought another male to our home?" I ask her quietly, though my voice echoes around the throne room like the unsaid threat that's tucked in the unnecessary question.

Because the answer is standing uncowed just beyond Susanna.

She lifts her shoulders, lets them fall. I grit my teeth, unwilling to let her sway me by swaying her obvious breasts. "He helped me—"

The red-eyed hunter is quick. Before anyone can stop him, he shifts so that he's standing in front of Susanna.

In front of *my mate*.

I am usually a gentle male. I only have to show my fierce side to remind my subjects why they do not want to cross their ruler. But now?

I rumble a warning sound deep in my chest. "What do you think you're doing, hunter?"

Susanna lays her hand on his arm. I'm already imagining tearing it from his socket when he eases himself from under her touch, putting a foot's length between the two of them.

I decide he can keep the arm… for now.

She doesn't seem to mind that he moved away

from her. Meeting my furious gaze, she says simply, "His name is Dagon."

I am aware. "Dagon of Caol. Hunter of his clan. Not your mate, Susanna."

"No," agrees Dagon. "But I am at her service."

Is he? "Explain yourself."

"Haures," begins Susanna.

The missing honorific catches the attention of every demon in my throne room. Even Dagon turns to look at her curiously, as though he's surprised that she would address the Lord of the Shadows so carelessly—even as he's standing between my duchess and I.

I shake my head. Not because she used my name… as my mate, she is the sole creature apart from the doppelseers that I'll allow it… but because I want the hunter to explain himself.

Then I will decide his fate.

It's what I must do as the duke. Susanna's male wants to challenge Dagon for even daring to think he can come between us, but Duke Haures? I must listen to him…

…and then I will sentence him to the shadows.

"Dagon. Don't make me ask again." When he doesn't answer quick enough for my liking, I snap. "Tell me. Why do you presume to stand between me and my mate?"

A hush falls over the room. I don't care. If I can't

trust my personal mage or members of my guard, then I have a much larger problem than hiding the truth of why I'm keeping a human in my realm. I fear that some of them… the ones I had tending to Susanna while I kept her locked up and safe in the dungeon… thought I was using the first law to keep a mortal woman as mine.

They didn't know that she was my one true mate —but now they do.

Dagon is the only one who doesn't seem surprised. Neither does he seem like he's concerned.

"She saved my life," he says at last, and through the thin bond connecting me to all of my subjects, I can sense he is prepared to sacrifice his to me even before he adds, "I owe her mine. I would pledge it to her until I can repay my debt."

"Oh," exclaims Susanna. She flaps her hands in front of her pretty mouth. "I know what he's trying to say. It's this thing we have back home. I've seen it on, like, every sitcom and cartoon ever. *Gill-uh-gan's Eye-land*," she says, an unfamiliar human word, followed by two I know, "and the flint and stones. It's a life debt. He thinks I saved his life. Now he wants to promise to be, you know, my bodyguard until he can save mine."

I am Duke Haures. I don't need anyone to keep my mate safe aside from me.

I glare at Dagon. "Is that so?"

He jerks his head. "There is a tie between us, your grace."

A tie?

A *bond*?

I snap my fingers, clicking my claws. "Glaine," I call. "Retrieve the demonkiller."

Susanna yips.

Sammael moves forward, proving that he is more than just a mage when he grabs Dagon by the shoulder, shoving him down to his knees. A pointed kick to his back has the hunter bowed over, forehead pressed to the tile.

At the same time, Glaine summons the blade I gave him when I made him the head of my guard. Only one of a handful of weapons charmed to eliminate an immortal creature, when I want to make a spectacle of an execution, I call on Glaine and his sword.

He positions it over the back of Dagon's neck.

"No," calls out Susanna. She jolts forward, dropping down next to Dagon. "You can't hurt him, Haures. Please."

Glaine's green eyes find mine.

I gesture for him to hold.

"My mate wants me to show mercy," I tell Dagon. "I want to know what happened in the shadows first. You say she saved you. Be honest, and she might save you again. What happened while she was in the shadows?"

"Your human… your mate," grunts out Dagon, keeping his head against the floor, "saved me when an arkoda got the better of me. I would've been its prey if she hadn't used fire and her shrill human noises to send it off—"

Susanna frowns at Dagon. "I wouldn't say I'm *shrill…*"

I'm not happy that the hunter is making my mate frown. At the same time, I think about that flash of danger coming through from her side of the bond. Was that when she was near an *arkoda*?

The arkoda doesn't come that close to the edge of the shadows. The large shadow beast usually lives farther into the darkness… unless it was hunting a hunter.

A hunter that nearly lost me my one true mate.

"You risked my female," I growl. "Why should I spare your life? Susanna might have saved it, but I am your ruler. Tell me why I should allow you to return to Caol."

Susanna's frown develops a sharp edge as she glares up at me. "Because I didn't go through the trouble of saving his behind only for you to chop off his head now, Haures. I had to use that damn flower to do it. Don't make my trip into that scary forest worthless."

My mate could ask me for anything and I would endeavor to give it to her if I can. She wants the hunter's life—saving him *again*—but it hits me at that moment what exactly she means.

She returned without the flower. She sacrificed it

to save Dagon, as though his life was worth tethering hers to mine for all of eternity.

Does Susanna know that that's what her gesture means? I don't think so, and that adds another layer to my emotions.

"You could have been free of me." I point at my human, swallowing my uncertain growl. "And still you returned without the flower?"

Does it matter that she used it to save Dagon from the arkoda? Or that, once the ashbalm flower's flame flickers out, she wouldn't be able to find another?

No.

Not to me.

And not to her, either.

Susanna's dark eyes meet mine as she slowly pulls herself back to her feet. In their depths, I see calm. I see bravery.

I see *defiance*.

Suddenly, my cock stirs beneath my linens. I want nothing more than to take it in hand, curving my fingers, my *claws* around it, drawing blood if only for a little release before I come in my grasp.

No.

No.

Truly, I want nothing more than to see my mate without her human coverings, laying her out on the crystalline floor, using my body to replace the tight fabrics as I nuzzle her with my tusks, spread open her cunt, and feed my aching length into her chilly body.

Once we finalize our bond by mating, Susanna will become immortal and grow warmer, more used to the Sombran fire. For now, it's a shock to my senses every time I dare brush against my mate, stealing her ice, and warming her with my heat.

But my Susanna is not my bonded mate. Not yet. And though I had to give her the choice to sever our tie, I know that I was right in understanding that I will never let her go when she tilts her pale face up at me and announces with a dare, "Who says I wanted to be free?"

In an instant, the rest of the throne room falls away. It's just Susanna. Only Haures. Our bond singing between us, growing thicker, stronger, unbreakable… at last, I open myself up to my mortal. My human. If I had any essence to give, it would be hers. Instead, I allow her in, knowing that it was her fearlessness in the face of my fury that sealed it for me.

She. Is. Mine.

Just then, the world narrows, surrounding only us two. The prophecies, the centuries of loneliness, the endless waiting… all of it twists into something that I've longed for, but never believed I could attain.

It's love.

It's possession.

It's need.

It's worship.

The gods granted me this female, and though I

will forever be grateful, this tiny slip of a human has the power to bring Duke Haures, Lord of the Shadows, to his godsdamn knees.

My mouth waters. My cock pulses against my linens.

My fingers twitch, desperate and eager to grab her and pull her onto my lap. I could feast on her cunt here, learn her deliciousness, send the demons gathered away, and christen Susanna—my duchess—in this very room.

I could, but I *can't.*

I nearly lost her. The story told by the hunter says that only he was in danger from the arkoda, that Susanna saved *him*, but what if the shadow beast had ended her at the edges of Sombra? I was not there. She is my light. My love. My everything… but I am the duke. I have a responsibility to my people.

To protect Susanna, I must keep the crown. But I can only keep the crown if I do my duty. There might be times when I cannot be with her, and though I may continue to hide her, it might not be such a terrible idea to allow this hunter to watch over her when I can't.

So long as he understands that she is *my* mate.

Rising up from my throne, I gesture for Firn to keep his place behind the throne. As though knowing what his liege requires, Sammael lifts his hands. I glance at him, nodding once, and he begins to conjure.

Susanna gasps.

Dagon's chin is pressed to the tile, Glaine's blade hovering over his neck.

I flick my claws at the guard. He lifts the demonkiller, twisting the sword once before disappearing it into the edge of his own shadows. As I stalk toward Susanna and Dagon, Sammael at my heels, Glaine slips away, joining Firn behind my throne.

I plant my feet in front of the bowed hunter. "Gaze upon your lord," I intone.

Dagon lifts his head just enough to do so.

"Do you pledge yourself to the mortal?"

Susanna starts forward. "He doesn't have to do that—"

Ah, my mate. But he *does*.

Dagon agrees. Without even looking over at Susanna, he firms his jaw, flashing his fangs. "I must. My honor demands it."

Smart demon.

Susanna uses her wee, flat teeth to nibble enticingly on her bottom lip. "But not forever, right? Only until you, like, save me? Settle the debt?"

Smart human. She does understand why Dagon would feel the need to save her in return, and not because she is an unmated female.

Because she isn't. I might not have formally claimed her, but I will.

I vow it.

For now, it is another vow I seek. "Do you vow to

watch over Susanna when I cannot until you either repay her, or you find a mate of your own to protect?"

Dagon's red eyes flare. I've given myself an additional clause to relieve Dagon of his duty, but I couldn't have done it any other way. I refuse to allow my mate to be in any danger, so there shouldn't be any time that Dagon will have to risk himself to save her life. But should he find his own mate… by then, I'll be formally bonded to Susanna. Her immortality will be another shield, and one I can't wait to bestow upon her.

Soon, I tell myself, waiting haughtily for Dagon's response.

"Yes," he grates at last, as though there could be any other response. But then he adds, "I vow it," and the roiling anger brewing inside of me since Sammael appeared with Susanna *and* Dagon finally settles.

He vowed it. There is no breaking a vow in Sombra, and every demon in our realm knows it.

I smile around my tusks. "Very well." Another gesture toward Sammael, who, by now, has finished conjuring another length of charmed chain. "Then off to the dungeon with you, Dagon of Caol."

CHAPTER 10

IN THE GARDEN

SUSANNA

So, as it turns out, the chains were for me.

Are you kidding?

I guess I should just be grateful that Haures didn't go ahead and execute Dagon in front of me. I tell you, I would've been way off when it comes to judging someone's character if he got that pissy green-eyed soldier guy to swing the sword. Haures is intimidating, a powerful ruler, but if he's my true love, he can't be a bloodthirsty monster, right?

No. He's supposed to be my goblin king. Or, rather, my demon duke. He can be cocky. So damn sure of himself. Tempting, too, in a way that I never would've expected before I manifested him. Enigmatic, and definitely manipulative.

But a monster? Haures might *look* like one, and I can't forget that he's tossed me to the dungeon *twice* now, but he… he can't be a monster. He's supposed to be my mate.

I mean, hey. He actually called me that before he… oh, yeah, *tossed me to the dungeon.*

I was really beginning to second-guess throwing the ashbalm flower at that bear thing. That arkoda. Whatever it was. All I can say for sure is that it would've gobbled Dagon up and I… I couldn't let that happen. Just like I couldn't let Haures pull a Queen of Hearts on the guy just because he had the bad luck to be in that dark forest the same time I was.

Then again, if I hadn't been there, he would've been lunch, so maybe I kind of get why he's so insistent on this whole 'life debt thing' after all.

When Haures announced that Dagon was being sent to the dungeon, I felt bad, but at least he got to keep his head. And then Haures gestured for Sammael to put the chains on *me*. Because I was being returned to the dungeon, and that was that.

There was no need to put Dagon in chains, too. He's already taking his vow—to me, and to Haures—super seriously. Wherever I go, he'll be right there if the demon duke can't, and since Haures only came down to retrieve me from the dungeon earlier today to feed me dinner, then send me out to get that flower, it's not like he's hanging with us.

To be fair, I should've expected this. A pity dinner and the offer to find the flower that would break our bond didn't change anything; not even him referring to me as his mate did, either, I guess. I'm still destined for the dungeon until he can figure out what to do with me.

Unless it's an oubliette, like in *Labyrinth.*

An oubliette… how did Hoggle describe it? A place to put people to forget about them? That sounds about right.

Sammael removed the chains once I was back in my cell again. Not so surprisingly, Dagon wasn't allowed to join me, though Glaine did say that Haures gave the demon permission to watch over me from the hall for now.

I didn't argue. Honestly? I didn't have it in me to. I went from thinking 'what-if'... what if Haures really is my true love… what if I get to stay in a world of demons, living in a palace instead of the dungeon… what if he's my Dan, and I get a family of my own like Mindy… but that all got dashed to pieces when I came back without the flower.

In a way, I thought that, without it, he'd have to finally admit that he's as drawn to me as I am him. And maybe I'm unlike any of the demons in this world, and that probably means I'm not like their demon women, either, but if I could look past his strange appearance, maybe he could look past mine.

Or maybe I have to realize that this isn't a fantasy movie where an immortal fae king falls for a silly human girl, willing to give up everything for her love. Maybe happy-ever-afters aren't real, and I'm stuck in Sombra, trapped in a jail cell, and I'll never hear Mindy's 'I told you so' when she finds out just how much trouble that damn book got me into.

And that's not even touching on how I had to promise that bodiless demon king my firstborn *and* something meaningful to me. At the time, I figured he couldn't take anything other than my scrunchie or my legwarmers since everything else was back on Earth—and with Haures acting like he was too good to want to bang it out with a human woman, I didn't have a firstborn in the cards.

But who said something meaningful meant an actual *thing*? What if it was the mate bond that Yelios decided to take captive until he got what he wanted?

Haures told me he was a bondmaster. What if all rulers of Sombra are? Could that creepy voice be powerful enough to take it from me? He nearly suffocated Dagon… I bet he could. It would be a calculated error, of course. Putting up a wall between me and the guy who is supposed to be my true love… not so sure how I'm supposed to get that firstborn he seems to want so badly if that's the case, but I have no idea how to make sense of any of this.

In the beginning, I decided to go along with this because, well, it's not like I had any other choice.

Being chained up and dragged into another realm through a mystical portal after I read a true love spell… yup. For my own sanity, I decided to treat this like I was a heroine in one of my favorite portal fantasy films. That way, I was all but guaranteed my happy ending.

Only this isn't a movie. It's real life. I have a family who has no idea what happened to me on the other side of that portal, and a true love whose first act was to use his power as ruler of this demon world to friggin' arrest me.

Some true love, huh?

Curling up on the bed, giving my back to the bars, I rub the heel of my hand against my chest. Is the bond there? It was. I know it was. True, Haures is so locked down, I've only felt slivers of it here and there, but it was enough for me to know that he was right. That spell brought us together, and I only wish I weren't the only one to see that.

Dagon had a muttered argument with Glaine before the guard left us together down here. I tried to drown it out, but voices carry in the dungeon. Unless I clapped my hands over my ears, it would be impossible for me to miss the grumpy guard telling Dagon that the duke insists on the bars to keep his mate protected.

Protected?

I'm a *prisoner.*

I'm pretty sure Dagon agrees. After Glaine

stormed toward the stairs, my new shadow moved toward the bars. I could sense him hovering, though I didn't look at him. He's had a way worse day than me, only in this mess because of his sense of duty and because Haures has decided that maybe I am his mate, but I can't help but be a little bitter that, if it wasn't for him, I might have been able to wash my hands of this whole thing and gone back home to Connecticut.

Is that where I want to be? No. Not really. My obsession with the *Grimoire du Sombra* has been such a huge part of my life. It's like I'm *supposed* to be here, and though I'd miss Amy and Mindy terribly, from the moment I first started translating the Sombran language printed on the pages, it just seemed *right.*

Now it's all wrong...

Dagon agrees with that, too. Mumbling softly from right outside my cell, he tells me that he'll get me out of here.

I can't see how, though I appreciate the sentiment.

At least someone sees how ridiculous it is to keep the five-foot-six mortal woman in a jail cell, as though she could ever be a danger or a threat to these seven-feet-tall immortal shadow demons.

Too bad it's not my supposed mate.

Dagon has figured out that I'm not going to be great company tonight. Or maybe he's a taciturn, quiet sort of hunter who appreciates the silence. Either way, he braces his bulk against the wall opposite of my cell, watching me closely without trying to engage in conversation.

Me? As bad as it sounds, I'm doing my best to pretend he's not there.

I really don't know how this is going to work. Will the guards feed him? How will he use that weirdo toilet in the corner of my cell? I have a cot, at least. Is he going to sleep on the floor?

How far will he go to be my own personal guard? What if I want privacy? I don't have to pee yet, but I will, and I just don't think I want to peel off my leggings in front of Dagon.

Would Haures care?

Do I want him to?

Ugh!

He's not your Jareth, Su. He's a demon, and he'll leave you here in the oubliette—

"My lord." That's Dagon's rough voice.

"I'm releasing you for the rest of the eve, Dagon." Crud. That's… that's *Haures*. "You watch the duchess when I cannot be with her. Tonight, I shall tend to my mate."

He will *what*?

Even more surprising than his unexpected appearance down in the dungeon is how it seems like he's really doubling down on this 'mate' business. Calling me 'duchess'? Correct me if I'm wrong, but a duchess is a duke's wife. Like Fergie, the new Duchess of York over in England.

I'm his human prisoner. I broke the first law by reading the *verus amor* spell, and I've paid for it these last few days by staying in a cell.

And *now* he's calling me 'duchess'?

He did earlier today. During lunch, right before he told me that I needed to go on a quick quest to find the ashbalm flower.

A duchess doesn't apologize…

How much do I want a bet that a duke doesn't, either?

I'd brushed him off then, too annoyed that he treated me like a toy that he could put away, then take off the shelf to play with at his pleasure. I wasn't a duchess. I wasn't anything. Sure, there was a bond, but there didn't need to be.

Even if I *wanted* there to be.

Referring to me as a 'duchess' in front of other demons… that's not all he does, either. I didn't know what to expect when he said he was going to 'tend' to me—and I would be lying if I said that that large silver sword that Glaine wielded earlier didn't pop into my overimaginative brain—but I figured that dinner, at least, was on the table.

Literally.

No. Guiding me to rest my hand on his massive

elbow after he opened the cell door and invited me out, the big demon shivered at the contact before leading me up the stairs. Once we hit the hall, he didn't bring me to the dining area. Instead, we returned to the throne room. The *empty* throne room.

I glance around. Every time I've been in here since my arrival in Sombra, Haures has had guards and mages and visitors. Not now. It's like they've all gone home for the night.

Shining down from the strange holes cut into the ceiling, a sliver of golden light mingles with the shade of blue overlaying everything in this space. You'd think it would create green. I mean, any kindergartner knows that's what you get when you put shades of blue and yellow together. Not in Sombra. Not in Haures's palace. The blue—the same color as his bright, glowing eyes—is so powerful that it takes over everything.

I thought it was because of the shimmering orbs dancing over crystal sconces that provide all of the light in the room. Nope. Because once Haures leads me across the room, tugging open a door I only just noticed with his free hand, I take one step outside and see that the blue light inside?

It's out here, too.

And that's not all…

Until Haures sent me into the shadow forest, I had no idea what Sombra looked like. I saw the fires in the distance, the ash made up of shades of black, white, and grey under my sneakers, and the way everything seemed to have a red tinge to it. Plus the heat. Can't forget the heat. I broke into a slight sweat immediately, and not even the cooler temp of the inky-black woods did much to help.

My first impression of his demon world seemed to fit every preconceived notion I had about where true demons lived. Like, this is totally Hell, right? From the horns and the red skin to the fires glowing in the distance… that part, at least, made sense.

If he had let me out into the courtyard of his palace first? I would've been way more confused.

The sky is a deep navy color. Overhead, one moon is gold. The other glows bright blue, just like Haures. And if you think I'm weirded out by the fact that I'm looking up at two moons? You haven't been paying attention. To me, that's just another reminder that I'm in a demon realm, one I need desperately when I walk outside and a chilled breeze—maybe seventy degrees instead of, like, *ninety*—blows past me.

The air is sweet. Fragrant. A mix of something floral, but more perfume-y—which definitely makes sense when I let go of Haures, drifting forward, taking in the beautiful garden in front of me.

There are flowers everywhere. In a world of fire and ash, I believed that the ashbalm flower with its flame for petals was the only sort of flower that grew in Sombra. Wrong. White flowers. Soft purple. Pale pink.

And blue.

So many beautiful blue flowers.

There's a fountain, too, with a trickle of water that tinkles as it hits the stone. I knew there had to be water somewhere. The strange tube-thing in my cell provided drinking water, even if the weirdo toilet didn't seem to flush at all; more of a black hole for you to do your business in than anything else. I get the feeling that rain isn't really a thing in such a fiery realm, but water… all living creatures need water, even immortal ones.

I tiptoe toward the fountain, running my fingers beneath the gentle flow. It's warm, like cranking up the temperature on the faucet when you're about to wash dishes, but not uncomfortable. In fact, if Haures wasn't standing right there, watching me take in the garden with a guarded expression on his rugged features, I might've stripped down and used the fountain to have my first bath in days.

But he is there, and when I glance over my shoulder at him, I notice that he's gone still. Is he holding his breath? I don't really get why immortal demons have to *breathe* in the first place, but since 'immortal' doesn't quite mean that they can't die—since I've gotten obvious proof that demons dying *is* a thing—that must be why he does.

Only he isn't, and when I reach deep inside of my chest, searching for our bond again, I actually find it. Maybe because Haures is right there, or because he's not keeping me out, I don't know… but I can sense how much he wants me to like the scene in front of me.

Luckily, I do.

"It's beautiful," I whisper into the quiet garden.

"It's yours."

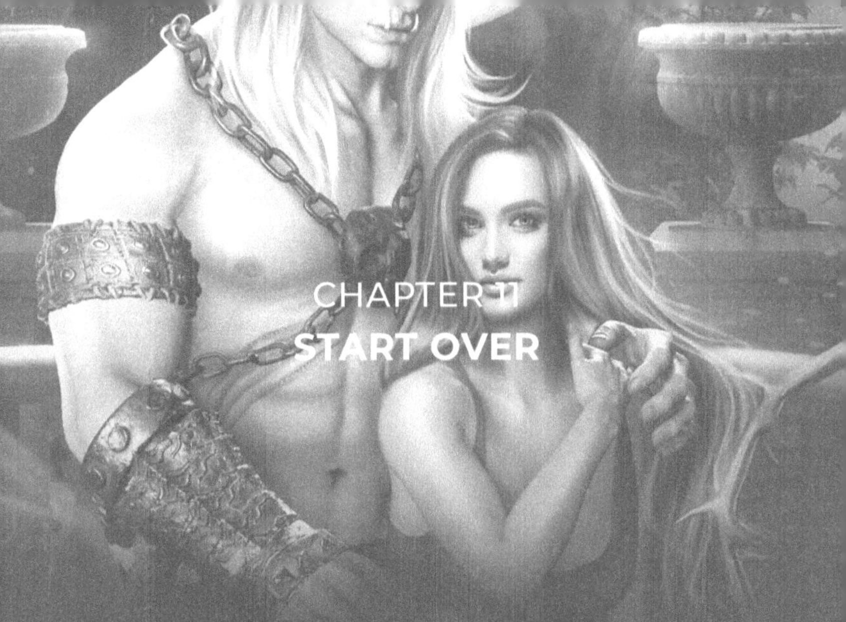

CHAPTER 11
START OVER

SUSANNA

"Me?" I whirl around, looking at Haures in surprise. His expression is flat, hands folded behind him as he watches me with intensity in his blazing blue eyes, though his lips are thinned, tusks rising up from the seam where they meet. "What do you mean, me?"

"Until you summoned me," he says, his voice unusually soft, "I knew one thing about my mate. A pair of seers told me twenty centuries ago that my mate, when she summoned me, would be human." A pause, and then a silent confession: "She would be born as a mortal."

I don't know what stuns me more: that he's known for—I quickly do the mat—*two thousand* years that, one day, he would have a human for mate, or that he doesn't seem as disgusted by the thought as I figured he was.

"You knew?" I ask. "And you waited for me?"

He jerks his head. A nod. "That is what we Sombrans do. I would accept no less than my one true mate, and I waited. More than that, I built Mavro to protect her. I built this garden to give her an oasis to enjoy… a place of beauty in a world of shadow. I built it with the promise of you in mind. And then—"

I gulp, sudden nerves lodging in my throat. "Yes?"

Haures takes a few slow, steady steps toward me. At least, I thought it was me. He takes a slight detour when he reaches me, ducking around my body so that he can bend slightly, plucking a flower from those growing near the fountain. It's blue. I get a fleeting glimpse of it as he lifts it up, and I swear the long, slender petals are the same shade of blue as Haures's eyes.

He tucks it behind my ear, nestling it in my hair.

"You are mortal, Susanna. I thought I understood what that would mean, and then you summoned me, calling me to your world. And I saw you. You are…" Haures takes a deep breath, shuddering it out. "Delicate. Breakable. Unique—"

My stomach tightens. "Weird," I say flatly. "To you demons, I mean."

"*Weird*," he echoes, as though the word doesn't quite translate into Sombran right.

"Unusual," I offer. "Different?"

"Perhaps. Different, yes, but also beautiful."

This time, my stomach lurches. Not out of a sense of rejection, though, but because Haures… did he just call me beautiful?

"And that's why this garden is yours. Because, like you, it's the only thing beautiful in my long, long life."

Darn. I want so badly to believe that he means what he says. Through the bond—our bond—it seems as if he's telling the truth, but how can he expect me to reconcile this demon to the frosty duke who sent me off into the forest barely a couple of hours ago?

"I thought you wanted to use the flower to break our bond. That you didn't *want* to have one with me."

Haures's eyes dim just enough to be noticeable. "Then that was my mistake. I wasn't being cruel. I was trying to save you."

I shake my head. "I don't understand."

"Then understand this: I rule my people. I rule Sombra. So worried that you might be in danger because of who I am, I tried to rule *you*… and Duke Haures I might be, but I never should've gone that far."

Nope. I still don't understand. "Haures?"

This time, when he lifts his hand, he strokes the edge of my jaw with his claw. Gentle… he's so friggin' gentle. I lean into his caress as he murmurs softly, "Until our bond is finalized, until you've promised yourself to me, until I've *claimed* you, you *are* mortal. You could be hurt."

"So could you," I retort. Just because he's immortal, that doesn't mean he can't die, and the idea that I could lose Haures so soon after finding out he's waited two millennia for me? I get a little loud. "Look at Dagon! He almost died twice today!"

"Demons *can* die," agrees Haures. "And locking you in the dungeon until you accept me won't keep you any safer, my mortal. And that's why Dagon didn't die. I grant him to you as your guard, watching you when I can't."

Okay. That calms me a little. "And when you *can*?" I ask.

His cheeks hollow as he sucks in a breath. "I won't let anyone harm you. Ever."

Later, I'll wonder what happened inside my brain. If I lost all common sense or something because making a move on a demon twice my size… probably not my best moment. What if he was just saying things he thought a girl wanted to hear, that my read on him was all wrong, that he *didn't* want me… I shove all of my second thoughts out of my head, hop up on the edge of the fountain—thank you, aerobics class!—before grabbing Haures's face in both hands.

Then, looking straight into his glowing eyes, I pucker my lips and kiss him.

Kissing around his tusks is easier than I thought, which is a good thing since I kind of didn't remember them at all until our mouths were smashed together. It becomes obvious almost immediately that Haures doesn't have any idea what I'm doing, but he'll let his mortal mate rub her lips all over his if it makes her happy. And since I do, urging him to respond a little, he eventually catches on to what I'm doing, moving his mouth a little beneath mine.

It's not a kiss with tongues or anything like that, but it's still a kiss, and I'm feeling a little dizzy when I finally release my hold on his jaw.

Haures blinks, too stunned to react, while I brace myself against his shoulder, holding onto him before I jump down from the fountain.

My sneakers hit the cobblestones, making a winding path through the garden with a slight slap. I tighten my pony, letting my hair settle over my shoulder as I look up at Haures, waiting for his reaction.

He just stares at me, tracing his claw over his bottom lip as though he can't believe that I did that to him.

A laugh bubbles up inside of me.

Holy moley, I think I stunned an ancient, immortal demon!

"What's the matter, Haures? Don't demons kiss?"

"Is that what that is called? A *kiss*?"

Again, he says that with an unfamiliar intonation, as though it's a word he's never used before.

I nod.

"But… why?"

Good question.

Um…

How do you explain a kiss?

I tuck a stray lock of hair behind my ear. "I don't know. It's something you do to show a guy you like him. That you care about him."

Suddenly, he's right there. Taking up every ounce of my personal space, he rests his big hand on my shoulder now.

I have to tilt my head up to see the confused expression on his face as he asks, "You care about me?"

Madonna, help me, but I do. I shouldn't. A stalwart romantic at heart, I was ready to go all-in as soon as he came back. He was my true love, right? I wanted so desperately to believe that my beloved spellbook wouldn't have led me wrong.

Of course, then my hopes were shattered when, instead of Haures being my very own Jareth, come to whisk me away to the Underground, he ordered me to an oubliette instead, keeping me in the dungeon for days before I had to go into the dark forest earlier—and, now, the garden…

I could say it was showing me the garden oasis that changed my mind. In a way, that has a lot to do with it. But what really tipped me over was his moment of vulnerability just now. When he admitted that he's waited *two friggin' thousand years* for me… I'd be a heartless human not to give him a second chance.

"Yes," I tell him, and the surprise that wells up in my chest… it's not mine. That's coming from the duke. Despite being open and honest with me, it's like he doesn't know how to act when the same sentiment is returned.

I'm Susanna Benoit. I was always the quiet girl with her nose in the book, but when I spent the last two years of high school carrying a spellbook around the school—because the cruel kids taunted me that it was one even before I ever realized that's what the pentacle meant—I became the weird girl.

So maybe that's why I had a bit of an off reaction when I thought Haures was calling me weird. I mean, I'm used to it. Nerd. Geek. Dork. I've heard it all, and I stopped letting it bother me—for the most part—more than a decade ago.

It doesn't bother me. Haures, though?

The big, powerful demon edges away from me—and I'm not so sure I like *that.*

"But I am… also different."

I raise my eyebrows. "And?"

"I am a beast, Susanna. To my people, I became the duke to hide the fact that I was an abomination."

Oh, Haures…

My heart breaks for him. It really does. If you asked me, his uniqueness makes him more attractive to me. I like his differences, from the way his large bottom teeth rise up instead of the other demon's fangs biting down past their lips to his long white hair and massive size. When he says he won't let anyone hurt me, I *believe* him.

I think back to what Dagon said to me earlier. About how taken aback he was by my overall humanness. Maybe that's why Haures and I are meant to be together. Neither one of us technically fit in in Sombra, but if he can call me beautiful, I can appreciate his uniqueness, too.

With a teasing grin, I say, "So you have white skin and white hair and tusks. Look at me. Dagon seemed disgusted by my…" What did he say? Oh, right. "...rounded ears, flat teeth, and dead eyes. If you don't mind me being a human, I don't care that you're different." I shrug. "In fact, I dig it."

I always thought that his glowing blue eyes were the only spots of color on Haures's face. Beneath the dual moons, I notice that his sharp cheeks are turning just pink enough to be noticeable.

For a hot second there, I think it's because he's slightly embarrassed—or maybe pleased—with the way that I hit on him. But then he blows air through his nose, snapping out, "I'll end him," and I know I got that way wrong.

"Why? Because he pointed out I was human when he's never seen one before?"

"Because he insulted my mate. He deserves to be returned to the shadows."

My cheeks are probably just as pink as I start to flush. Now this? This is the side of Haures that just might be my true love.

Even so, I say, "I appreciate it, but please don't. Not when I went to so much trouble to save his skin in the first place."

He grunts, and I assume that's Haures's way of agreeing that he won't threaten Dagon anymore when he brushes his thumb against his lip again.

"Have you *kiss*ed many males?" he asks, and it hits me that his mind is still stuck on our kiss.

Swallowing my smile, I pat his chest. His jealousy shouldn't be such a turn-on, but it is. It totally is. "None that matter," I tell him. And it's true. I'll treasure each of those pecks, those sloppy, wet kisses, but they weren't with my true love. They weren't with my demon duke.

Haures takes my hand, swallowing it in his. Proving that he was paying attention, he lifts it up, pressing his lips—and, okay, his tusks, too—against my wrist. With his other hand, he strokes his chest.

"You are my mate," he rumbles, "and once you've accepted me as yours, I will have my finest artist carve your name in my chest so that all of Sombra knows that you're mine."

"So… if you're getting a me tattoo, does that mean I won't have to spend all of my free time in the dungeon now?"

I meant it as a tease. Something changed in this

garden, and if Haures decided to take this moment and poop on it by crushing my hopes, breaking my trust, and treating me as a prisoner again… I don't think I could get over that. He has to know that; from my reactions, and whatever he can sense coming from me through our bond the same way that I can pick up on flickers of his emotions.

"I will protect you," he vows. "If I must keep you hidden from my people, I will. But, I promise you, Su, that I will never deny that you *are* my mate. But the dungeon… you will never set foot in there again. As you are my mate, the first law hasn't been broken. You will join me in the palace."

I hear the promise ringing true in his solemn words. I guess that's as good as I can hope for, and the idea of joining Haures in the beautiful palace is definitely better than the gloomy jail cell.

I look forward to getting to know Haures. Not just the demon duke, but the guy he really is when he doesn't have to be the hardass ruling over his realm.

Moving into Haures, enjoying the way he looms over me, I ghost my fingers over the scars on his side.

It took me until just now to notice them. In the throne room, the blue light hides a lot. It's probably on purpose; I can't imagine a powerful demon duke being proud to show off any hint that they weren't infallible. He's immortal. I don't think I saw any scars on any of the other demons… until I looked over at him in this garden, the two moons of Sombra overhead illuminating his striking image.

Though I bet he'd deny it, Haures is obviously insecure about how different he looks from the other demons. The way he called himself a beast just now… it bothers him that he rules a land of shadows, calling himself the lord of them, but he is the opposite of them.

His scars seem to be as unique as the rest of him. They are four slash marks that start on his left side before wrapping partway around his bulk to his back. His skin is so white—and I mean *white*, not peachy or pinky like white humans—that it's almost impossible to notice the slight variation in the empty color.

Unless you're right there. Unless Haures lets you close.

"You've already been marked," I point out. "If you don't mind me asking, what happened?"

"You may ask me anything, Susanna." He glances down, looking at the scars as if seeing them for the first time—or remembering the circumstances of how he received them. Then he says a word that I've only learned today: "It was an arkoda."

"That thing that was trying to gobble up Dagon."

He nods. "You see, I, too, was left to the shadows." Again, his eyes dim over. "It's where demons go to die. Or, when you're a young spawn that is different from the others, it's where your kin abandon you to hide their shame."

I don't have to ask if that's what happened to him. The bitterness in his voice is echoed by the emotions coming down our bond.

It doesn't last, though. Showing the same grit and determination that saved him from the arkoda and led him to be the demon duke of Sombra, Haures shuts down that bitterness, a fierce promise reaching me instead.

He tucks the tip of his claw under my chin. "This world is full of dangers, duchess. But know this: nothing is as dangerous as your male."

Your male.

My mate.

Haures… he's claiming me.

You know what? This is going to be me claiming him right back the only way I know how.

This… what we have won't be easy. I mean, we definitely didn't get off on the right foot. He's a demon, I'm a human, and that's the least of our worries… but you know what's good about having an immortal demon for your true love? Depending on how long I get to stick around—and something tells me that, so long as I stay with Haures here like he wants, it might just be forever—then we have a long, long time to make up for a crummy first impression.

Why not start now?

"Call me Su," I tell him, for the first time giving him permission to use my nickname. "Not duchess, okay? Just Su."

Haures stands up, his full height making him seem even more imposing than before. I'm not afraid of him, though. If anything, it's cute that he thinks that he can attempt to intimidate me after admitting that everything he's done so far was to treat me like his mate.

And Haures will never, ever hurt his mate.

"Are you refusing to be my duchess?" he booms.

Cute. I'm sure that would scare his subjects, but I'm not his subject.

I'm his true love.

"I'm not saying that. Not at all. It's just… hey. You and me, let's start over. Okay?" Stepping away from him so that there's just enough space between us, I shove out my hand toward him. "My name is Susanna Benoit. I like Bon Jovi, David Bowie, and *Labyrinth* is an awesome movie that never leaves my VCR. Books are my best friends, and I spent almost half my life translating one. I read a spell, hoping it would work, and it did." When Haures's sudden fury transforms to adorable confusion, I slip my hand into his huge mitt, pumping my arm so that he has to shake it. Then, with a small smile, I peer up at him and ask, "You?"

For a moment, I think he's going to give me one of those haughty shakes of his head. Maybe think his new pet human is being silly, and change the subject to something involving more dead demons that pissed him off.

But then, whether it's because he's actually trying, or he's using the bond to learn me the same way as I'm researching him… and I am an *excellent* researcher… Haures changes his grip on my hand, cupping my fingers gingerly.

He shakes my hand again, gently, all while being careful not to jab me with his pointy claws. "I am Duke Haures, Lord of the Shadows, Sombra's ruler. My people address me as 'your grace'. You should call me *yours*. I like your"—His forehead furrows, obviously searching for an unfamiliar word—"*horsetail*."

With his free hand, he uses his claws to fiddle with the end of my pony, then solemnly says, "And even if your eyes are dark and don't shine like mine, they are beautiful. *You* are beautiful."

I gulp, another lump lodged in my throat. "Haures…"

He shushes me softly. "I waited nearly my entire existence… more than twenty centuries… for you to find me. And now that you have, I will never let you go. You made your choice today when you returned without the ashbalm flower. I make mine now. I call you mine, my mate. My duchess. My Su."

Know what? It's not the exact 'promise' that I translated in the *Grimoire du Sombra*, but right now, it doesn't matter. Haures has claimed me, well and truly claimed me as his with his words and the heated look on his face, and for the first time since I summoned him to Connecticut, the bond in my chest isn't tugging me toward him, trying to make us both understand that we *are* true loves.

Here, in this blue garden, standing beside Haures, I am at peace, and that's because I'm with him.

I will miss Mindy. Amy, too. Dan… eh, whatever, but my friends… my family… my *book* that's probably still abandoned in my empty house… I'll miss them. They'll forever have a piece of my heart.

But the rest of it?

I plan on giving to my one true love, so long as he'll have it.

CHAPTER 12
I NEED YOU

SUSANNA

So… I'm still a secret.

I can't really complain. He's gotten better at needing to hide me constantly. The maids and cooks know I exist now; I finally get a balanced plate of food instead of just meat. Most of the guards that have constant access to me are aware that Haures has a human mate. Glaine, who I go out of my way to avoid, and a handful of others. Haures's mage, Sammael, seems more and more fascinated by the mortal world he visited when Haures instructed him to join him so that Sammael could put me in chains. Because Haures explained it was on his orders—and that he did so to keep me contained during travel between realms since he expected his appearance to frighten his mate way more than it ever did me—I decided not to hold it against Sammael. Besides, he's the only one who doesn't seem to hold my mortality against *me*.

Well, except for Dagon, that is.

Even so, I can tell the hunter is still iffy when it comes to me being a human woman. He's satisfied Haures's jealous side, proving that he's only devoting himself because of his life debt and not because he's into me. Somehow I've found myself saddled with a taciturn bodyguard who barely speaks. It's like pulling fangs here to get him to call me 'Susanna' on the rare occasion that he does.

To those that know about me, Haures isn't shy in claiming that I'm his mate. I'm precious cargo these days. A fact he reiterates by installing me into my own bedroom right next to his, with a huuuge featherbed, and a closet full of the most gorgeous dresses, each one in my size.

Turns out, these pair of psychic demon twins told him that, one day, his mate would be a human. Since he didn't quite know what to expect, he wasn't able to provide clothes for me until I summoned him, and he —courtesy of this unique bond between the bondmaster and his one true mate—knew my size instinctively, down to the fact that I wear a size eight shoe.

Did it matter that he had no reference for what a 36C bra or size eight shoe meant? Not at all because he was able to describe me so precisely, a legion of talented demoness seamstresses whipped me up a wardrobe and shadow-woven boots during the three days I was in the dungeon.

I don't know what was the bigger relief: being able to change my clothes at last, or that I got to take the longest soak in a charmed bathtub with perfectly steaming water and soap that left me smelling like cotton candy.

I'm being pampered these days. And if it kind of sucks just a little bit that I seem to spend more time with quiet Dagon than I do Haures, I deal with it. We share meals, and he invites me to watch him rule whenever the throne room is empty of anyone who doesn't know his secret. Plus, you know… *virgin.* I've been living as Haures's duchess for weeks now, close to a 'cycle' as my mate refers to a month, but while Sombra demons don't need half as much sleep as a human woman does, I've yet to sleep with my mate.

Haven't banged him yet, either.

I thought the bond gave me a little relief from the tug I constantly feel toward Haures after we both agreed to give this mate thing a try. And it did for a couple of days. Slowly but surely, though, it started to creep back in. A flush here. A hint of fever, there. My body was achy. My boobs heavy. My pussy on *fire.*

I wanted my mate to be my mate in all the ways that matter, and it seems like the bond agrees.

I remember how Haures fondled himself after the shockingly erotic image of him feasting on my pussy popped into my brain. It was definitely his fantasy, not mine, though I'd be lying if I said I didn't imagine what it would be like with Haures's warm mouth on my most private of parts.

He's being careful, though. Treating me with kit gloves. As though he wants to make up for my less-than-stellar welcome, he's not rushing me into anything. So long as I accept that I'm his mate, he's happy to move forward at this snail's pace.

Me? Not so much, but I refuse to be pushy, either. If he wants to wait to take this mating of ours to the next step, I can. So long as I do the waiting in my cushy bedroom or hang out in the gorgeous garden he gave to me, I'm okay.

I like the garden. It's where I had my first kiss with Haures, and where he goes to find me whenever he is hungry and desperate for another.

You know what I like even better?

The royal *library*.

That's right. Haures has a library in this castle, and like the garden, he tells me that it belongs to me now.

If that's not a panty-dropper, I don't know *what* is.

He also took me to the School of Mages to show me their library. I'm delighted to discover that, before it was bound into the *Grimoire du Sombra* alongside many of the school's spells for their students, the *verus amor* spell—also known as the matefinder spell—was a scroll in that very library.

I wonder about taking a quick trip to Connecticut,

maybe retrieve the book and leave a goodbye note behind for Mindy. I hate to think what would happen if the grimoire fell into the wrong hands, and I do everything I can not to think about how freaked out Min must be by now about my disappearance.

I tried mentioning it to Haures once. When he understood the reasons behind my wanting to open a portal between my old world and this one, he lost his emotionless edge, promising me that I could… but only after we were formally bonded. Nothing I said could persuade him otherwise, so I dropped it.

That's not the only topic that my haughty mate refuses to discuss, either.

In the days that followed my trip into the shadows, I try to talk to him about it. He knows about Dagon, obviously. What he doesn't know? Is about the deal I made with Yelios—but he won't let me tell him, either.

I agreed to be his mate. Now that I have, Haures needs to understand *what* I promised to the old demon king, and why I did it. I would never risk our child, but when I never believed there would *be* one… no. He needs to know, and he needs to hear it from me, not from what he infers from the scattered emotions and thoughts that trickle down my side of our bond to his…but he absolutely refuses to hear a single word about it, cutting me off whenever I bring up my trip to the shadows.

I know why, too. He's stupidly worried that what

I'm trying to do is ask for a chance to retrieve another ashbalm flower. As I've since learned, only one appears every cycle of the gold moon—the second, smaller moon that has significance to the Sombra demons—which is why I couldn't simply grab a spare after I destroyed that first one to save Dagon.

I can't get him to understand that I don't want to sever our bond. I want to *finalize* it. But as long as Haures feels like he needs to protect me… I'm stuck again.

Even worse?

I don't know if I'll ever truly be his duchess.

WHENEVER I GET TOO ANXIOUS, ALONE IN MY bedroom or reading a book in the library, I tend to gravitate toward the garden.

Dagon, too, of course, though I'm getting used to having a seven-foot-tall shadow trailing me. I've made it my mission to turn my bodyguard into my friend, and while it's slow going, I've been making progress over the last few days.

He even cracked an almost-smile when I made a joke yesterday!

For now, I've got my dress curled up beneath my butt, sitting carefully on the edge of the fountain. I kind of have to; be careful, that is. The seamstresses got my size dead-on, but I guess undergarments aren't really a thing here because… whoops. No bras. No panties. My shadow boots—and that's so friggin' cool that my boots are made of *shadow*—are comfortable enough that I don't need socks. It's just me and my dress, and I'm just grateful the bodice has enough support that my boobs aren't flopping everywhere.

Dagon is standing at the far end of the garden, his back straight, his horns pointed up at the sky. His gaze is forward, though if I even move so much as an inch, his head jerks, making sure I'm safe. Otherwise, he's not there, paying more attention to the full gold moon overhead than he does me.

One day, I hope I'll get used to *that*. I don't see how I'm in any danger here in the garden, and I'm sure Dagon would rather return to his home village instead of watching me play 'he loves me, he loves me not' with the blue flowers, but for now, he's refusing to leave my side unless Haures is near.

I tried to point out that he's right there, on the other side of the door leading out to the garden. Who knows? I could scream, and he probably would hear me. The garden is probably the safest part of the whole capital since no one else comes out here except for me, Dagon, and Haures.

Of course, right as I have that exact thought, an unfamiliar green-eyed demon suddenly appears. I didn't even see him come through the door, though he's in his shadow form. For all I know, he zipped up and out of the hole in the palace's ceiling before landing just beyond the fountain.

I make a small sound of surprise.

Immediately, Dagon is at my side, flexing his claws, baring his fangs at the intruder. "Tropp. What are you doing so close to the duchess?"

Tropp. Right. I see it now. Even in his shadow form, his left horn is slightly shorter than the other.

His green gaze flickers toward me, dismissing me just as easily. I ignore it. Most of the guards refuse to accept that I'm going to be the duchess since Haures and I haven't bonded yet, and the duke's broad chest is still without a Su tattoo.

Whatever.

Tropp clears his throat. "Dagon. His grace has requested your presence in the throne room."

"My loyalty is to the duchess," Dagon says flatly. "I will not leave her alone even if Duke Haures demands it."

Oh, jeez. Talk like that will have Dagon on his knees again, Glaine's killer sword swinging over the back of his neck.

Tropp would see to it, too. The guards don't like that a mere hunter from one of the smaller villages in Sombra has taken a position that they feel, by rights, should've gone to one of them. Given the chance, they'd get rid of Dagon. I'm sure of it.

No.

I shift in my seat, turning toward Dagon. "Go," I

tell him gently. "I'll stay right here in the garden. See what my mate wants. I'll be fine."

Poor Dagon looks torn. On the one hand, he means it when he says that he's here to take care of me. On the other, his loyalty better be to Haures first in public because, otherwise, that's a shadow offense and even *I* know that. I could probably save him again, but then I'll *never* get rid of him.

And I like Dagon. I do. He's the puppy I never had as a kid, but I wouldn't mind five seconds to myself for once.

"Go," I tell him, a little more oomph in my voice. "Really."

The order does what it's supposed to: Dagon nods, then strides toward Tropp.

"I will return," he says solemnly to me.

I smile.

Trust me, Dagon. By now, I don't doubt it.

Tropp doesn't even give me a second look. Leading the hunter-turned-bodyguard toward the throne room door, it's as though I've ceased to exist to the guard.

To Tropp, maybe.

But the red-skinned, spiky-haired, one-horned demon that seems to take his place?

Nah. As he stalks out of the garden's furthest shadows the moment Tropp and Dagon are gone, it's clear to me that I have *all* of his attention.

I don't want it. There's something crazed in his

vibrant purple eyes. He's hunched slightly, racing right toward me, and I'm barely standing before he's mere inches away from me.

He smells sickly sweet, a hint of wispy shadows coming from the tips of his pointed ears, his fingers, his elbows adding a burnt aroma to it. Like when you try to make homemade caramel and keep it on the pot too long.

My lips twitch, a quick smile. "Hello. I'm Susanna. Can I help you?"

His eyes flare, going from purple to white and back. From what I've learned, purple means 'magic'. *Mage*. He's a spellcaster.

And I'm in trouble.

"I see," he whispers, his voice low and ragged. "The gods grant me visions and I *see*… I see that you will lead to the end of Sombra. Your arrival in our world will bring about its ruin." Another flicker, white, then purple, then white this time. "I can't allow you to destroy our people."

I hold up my hands, heart starting to pound wildly as he leans into me, spitting on my face as he hisses at me. "No. You've got it wrong. I wouldn't—"

I never get the chance to tell him what I would or wouldn't do. Faster than I expected—and I should've known better because Sombra demons can be *quick*—he wraps his big paws around my neck and squeezes.

He closes my throat off. I gasp, unable to get one

last breath. He squeezes harder. Black spots form at the corners of my eyes.

I claw at his hands, but I'm human. I'm *mortal*. My fingernails don't do any damage to him. Even if they did, all he would have to do to heal would be turn to shadow before returning to his solid form, and he'd have nothing to show I even tried to fight back.

That's why Haures has scars when no other demon does. He has his own unique abilities, but he doesn't heal the same way. And me?

I'm a goner.

Haures…

In the seconds before I'm about to lose consciousness, my life really does flash before my eyes. I think of Mom. Of Mindy. Of Amy.

And then, my soul crying out to his, I reach for Haures.

When the pressure on my throat releases mere moments before everything turns black, I have a moment where I think that I skipped the whole unconscious stage. That I went straight to Heaven or something because, suddenly, there is Haures.

Ferocious and glorious, his blue eyes blazing in fury, his white hair streaming behind him beneath the gold moonlight…

He's here. My mate is here.

The howl of rage he lets out brings me back around. I'm not dead. I'm gasping, on my knees, sucking in breath after breath, rubbing my neck. I'm *alive*—

But that crazed seer won't be for much longer.

It's the bond. I can sense Haures's fear that I was hurt, anger that I was left vulnerable, and that same rage that one of his people tried to hurt his mate. As the demon duke, there was nothing else to do. He's judge, jury, and, in this case, executioner.

He doesn't ship the seer off to the shadows. He doesn't retrieve Glaine for the sword, either.

Instead, picking the seer up by the throat, dragging him off of the cobblestones where he must've thrown him after ripping him away from me, Haures does exactly what the rogue demon did: he wraps his hand around his throat and squeezes.

Flames burst from his fingers. Gentle flames, delicate flames, flames that lick at the seer's flesh. I can't imagine they would really hurt a demon who calls this world home, but the moment his eyes fade back to purple and he sees that he's both facing off against Haures *and* that my mate's hand is on fire?

The seer starts to beg. To plead. To demand mercy.

In response, Haures only squeezes infinitely tighter until the seer's entire body is engulfed in the slightly transparent flames.

Releasing him, the seer hits the cobbles with a loud *thud*. He doesn't stop-drop-and-roll or do anything to put out the flames. As though accepting his fate, he just curls up at Haures's feet.

Haures's expression is terrible. "You tried to harm my mate. I'm not that merciful."

He clicks his claws together. I hear a soft *pop*, gasping when the seer… he… he's *ash.* Like, *just* ash. He doesn't even burn all the way. With a burst of Haures's magic, he turns my attacker into a pile of greyish-white ash and nothing else.

As soon as he has, wild blue eyes search for me. "You called for your male through our bond. I felt you needing me. Thank the gods I reached you in time. But did I? Tell me, Su… tell me you are unharmed."

My throat's gonna hurt like heck tomorrow, but I'm alive. He *saved* me just like he promised he would. "I am."

"Good."

Not quite the response I expected, but okay—

Whoa.

"Haures? Haures!"

My demon mate just crossed the distance between us, hefting me up, swinging me around, searching for somewhere else to place me once he's done. I figured on my boots, away from the pile of ash, that would work… and then he tilts me back with his impressive strength, laying me out on the cobblestones surrounding the fountain.

"Apologies, Su," he says, "but… the gold moon…

and almost losing you… I cannot help it. Your mate requires his female."

I see that.

And you know what? I'm a-okay with it, too.

My close brush with death might've just made me screwy. Nearly being choked to death… I don't know. I shouldn't be so turned-on by the fact that my mate just barbecued another demon in front of me, but he's right. Something about the full gold moon had me fantasizing about Haures all afternoon, and if that's what he needs to blame this sudden desire on, sure. Let's go with that.

Still, I can't help but tease him. As he works single-mindedly to get my skirts out of his way, I say, "I thought dukes don't say sorry."

"No. I said that a *duchess* never apologizes. But a demon duke will do anything to get to his mate's sweet cunt."

I grip my skirts with both hands, yanking them up so that my lower half is bared to Haures. "Well, damn. All you had to do was say please."

"Please." It's a whisper. It's a groan. It's a *prayer* to the Sombran gods, and a plea to the mortal woman he has on her back. "*Please.*"

I let my hair cushion my head, staring up at the gold moon winking back at me. "I'm yours, Haures. I'm *yours*."

One thing I've learned since living in Sombra? Every happy-ever-after is going to look different.

Mine? Mine's going to be with a fierce demon who comes when I subconsciously call him, kills for me, then buries his face in my pussy, while the ash of the demon he killed sits just beyond his bare foot.

And I wouldn't have it any other way.

CHAPTER 13
VOW

HAURES

I have lived for more than two thousand years. Nearly twenty-four centuries, and I mean it when I say that the hardest thing I've ever had to do was pull myself away from Susanna's welcoming cunt after she allowed me to *kiss* it.

As a young spawn, moving from village to village, hoping there would be one that accepted me after my own mother left me to the shadows, I had witnessed a demon male taking his demoness many times. From my youthful spying, I understood that a cock's purpose is to lodge inside my mate's cunt, for pleasure and to eventually create a spawn.

But there was more to mating than just such a union. Though demons don't usually mate with their mouths, I have seen a male do such a thing while his demoness pulled up her skirts. I've always wondered what my mate's cunt would taste like, and now I know.

It is sweeter than demon wine, and even more addicting.

Hearing my beloved Su keen my name, crying out in pleasure as my *kiss* brought her to completion on my face… I only drew away when she begged me to because her wee body was too sensitive for more of my hunger. But though I have never claimed a female before, all males have instincts. My cock was so hard, it could've bored holes through the cobblestones of her oasis garden. I even thrust, trying to tame my own need because I knew… I knew as though Damien came to me with a riddle of my future… that, should she spread her thighs and tell me to feed her my cock, I would have without a moment's hesitation.

But I could not. To do so during the night of the gold moon… the gods of Sombra can be very wicked. They give us an immortal life, but for many demons, it can take centuries or even millennia to find our one true mate—and that's assuming we ever do before an endless life becomes too weary and we, like Yelios did, disappear to the shadows. And they promise us spawn to continue our lines, but should we mate during that eve, our females will be with child every time, whether we want to grow a family or not.

And then, to make it so that a demon does take

his female on the night of the gold moon, the desire to do so is damn near irresistible…

In all my years, I never contemplated giving myself over to the shadows. I survived them as a spawn before Yelios had ever slunk into them, and after I took his throne and he vanished, I never set foot in them again.

I should have. Maybe then I would've known that he lurked there still before he could trick my sweet human mate into offering up our firstborn child.

I don't blame Susanna. She didn't know, and if I hadn't hidden so much from her after I stole her to Sombra, she might have been better prepared not to barter with a demon such as Yelios. The gods will hold her to her vow, but I've learned my mate, both through our bond and because she is most pleased to talk with her male when my duties are done and I can spend time with her.

For nearly a cycle, she has tried to find the words to tell me what happened in the shadows. She doesn't know that Dagon already confessed what Susanna sacrificed for his sake, just like she doesn't understand the lengths to which our bond connects us. There isn't anything I don't know about this female—and that was why I had to put the distance between me and my mate.

Because she would've welcomed me, inviting me to mate her and claim her, not knowing that the gold moon would fill her with the child destined for Yelios…

A child born of two worlds,
belonging in both, belonging to none,
will bring with them rain,
and the fires of Sombra will be forever done.

Even if she hadn't made her impulsive vow, I could not risk bringing a child into this world, knowing that it could bring about the end of it. I only just found my Su. I want eons with her before the doppelseers' prophecy might possibly steal her away from me.

So, for the night of the gold moon, I had to pull away, lifting up my sated, trembling mate, carrying her through the throne room where Tropp tried to keep Dagon from returning to his mistress.

I could've passed her off to Dagon to guide Susanna to her quarters before I relocate hers to mine. But then I once again notice the red marks on her throat, a reminder that Bandu—a seer from Caim's village in Dunkel—had been throttling her when I received her call through our bond. Fury rages anew, and before the flames that I've long kept hidden burst free of me for the second time that night, I call out to Glaine.

"Seize Tropp," I tell him, my voice as icy as Susanna's cunt was when I took my first lap of her flesh before my tongue warmed her up. Only once we're bonded will she be more suited to Sombra's clime, and as I clutch her to me, I know that that will be mere days away. Once the gold moon wanes… "Keep him here until I return. Dagon? Follow. You will guard my mate after I lay her down to rest so that I can attend to matters here."

Dagon nods, moving a few paces behind us, ready to follow. Glaine grips Tropp's arm, the other guard baring his fangs, though he doesn't fight against the head of my guard's hold.

Why would he when he knows that his duplicitous nature has been revealed?

To let a seer into Susanna's garden… that would take a member of my palace guard. And who brought Dagon to me, claiming I requested his presence?

Tropp did.

And, soon, he will join Bandu as ash—

"Haures?" Her voice is dozy, with a hint of concern. She's coming down from her heights of pleasure, something I do not want. Let my demons scent her need and their lord's musk all over hers. Let them know she is *mine*… "Is everything okay?"

I squeeze her to me gently. "Everything will be just fine, my mate."

I am Duke Haures. Lord of the Shadows. Ruler of the Flames.

Susanna of Earth's claimed mate.

Everything will be fine because I will make sure of it.

LATER THAT NIGHT—AFTER I SENT FOR CAIM TO return to Mavro so that he can clean up the ashen remains of the traitorous seer and the soldier, both of his clan—I returned to Susanna's current quarters, eager to at least see for myself that my mate is doing well after her scare.

I want to apologize. I am her male. Her mate. I will always go to her when she calls, but no matter how I try to protect her, there's a possibility that danger can find her. In a way, I am almost grateful that the gold moon is this eve. Before I bond Susanna to me forever, I need her to understand just what it would mean to be tied to Haures for the rest of her existence.

I have conquered many enemies. For Su, I will conquer them all. But I never want to feel that same horror, the fear that I was too late to save her. Making her immortal would alleviate some of that terror for me, but to claim her without giving her another chance to change her mind after Bandu attacked her… it would be as selfish as not giving her the opportunity to search for the ashbalm flower.

And while I can admit that that was also a rare mistake from the ruler of Sombra, she chose me then.

Hopefully, she'll still choose me now.

When I enter the room, she's wearing a nightdress, showing off her enticing human body. I know that she does not do so to tempt her male. It wouldn't even be necessary; I always hunger for my mate. But that she's wearing a nightdress and not tucked under the blanket that she requested despite how warm Sombra must seem to her… she was waiting for me.

I check the bond, inwardly wincing when it's clear that she did not do so because she wanted to resume our mating.

No. Susanna wants to talk, and while I do, too, she wants to once again confess something that she shouldn't be so nervous to admit. And because she *is* nervous, I don't stop her before she can begin, like I have ever since she returned from the shadows. I thought I was being an honorable male. I don't blame her for the way she promised Yelios her firstborn, though I can sense that Susanna blames herself and is fearful of how I will react at learning the truth.

But I already *know* the truth. I know because I know *her*, just like I have to begrudgingly respect that she made her vow to save one of my subjects. Dagon cannot help that he is male any more than Susanna can help her kind and brave heart. She saved him at her own loss, and that makes her as honorable in my eyes as I yearn to be.

So when nervous hands fiddle with the hem of her skirt, I stride across the room, joining her on the edge of the bed, and listen as she tells me everything that happened during her trip to the shadows. I stay quiet, letting my presence and my echo down our bond assure her that she did nothing wrong.

Still, she must think that she did because, once she finished her confession, she hurriedly says, "I don't have to. I mean, if we ever… if I *have* a kid… there's gotta be a way to keep Yelios from taking him or her from us. Right?"

There is nothing more I want in that moment than to scoop Susanna up in my embrace and tell her that is true. That our spawn will be ours, and that I would end Sombra myself before I let the deranged demon king claim the child.

But I am Duke Haures.

As powerful as I am, I am no match for the gods.

How can I be when they blessed me with my mortal? To question their judgment might mean they take her away from me as easily as they granted me her glory.

I would fight Yelios, I cannot fight the gods.

So, with a voice solemn with regret, I tell her the truth: "In Sombra, the gods will always make it so that you stand by your vow. Any vow, my mate. Once given, they are unbreakable."

"Oh." The saddest sound in all my existence will forever be the soft sob she lets out after I crush her hopes… until she follows it with a mumbled, "I'd understand if you decide you don't want to be my mate anymore. I mean… we haven't really done the deed yet or anything, and if you want to have kids with someone who didn't stupidly promise theirs away, I don't blame you."

My heart stops. For a moment, I'm sure she's rejecting me—but she isn't.

She's preparing herself for me to reject *her*.

No. I can't do that.

I *won't* do that.

Reaching into her lap, I take her trembling, tiny, icy hands in mine. And then, with as much emotion as I can, I promise, "My soul will be yours. My heart is in your hands. Our lives will be forever intertwined—"

Susanna tilts her head back, looking up at me as I peer lovingly down on her. "Haures? What… what are you doing?"

"Me? I am making my vow to you, my duchess. The gods will hold me to it, but they don't need to. When I give you my mating promise, it's because I mean it with every inch of my battered, scarred, beastly body. Understand me, mortal?"

She makes a strange human noise, different from the sob. It is… I reach into our bond, searching for the human word. Ah. She *hiccups*, and I smile around my tusks.

Susanna returns it, her dim eyes growing shiny with wet. Lifting my hand, leaving her two nestled in my other, I swipe the wet away gently with the edge of my claw.

She leans into my caress.

My heart swelling inside of my chest, I continue the mate's vow that will make it so that I can never promise myself to another. What other? I will only ever want this female… "I give myself to you, Su. I give you *everything*."

"Ditto."

In human, that means she accepts my mate's promise—and she reciprocates it.

Susanna is *mine*… and I will prove it to the both of us once the gold moon is over.

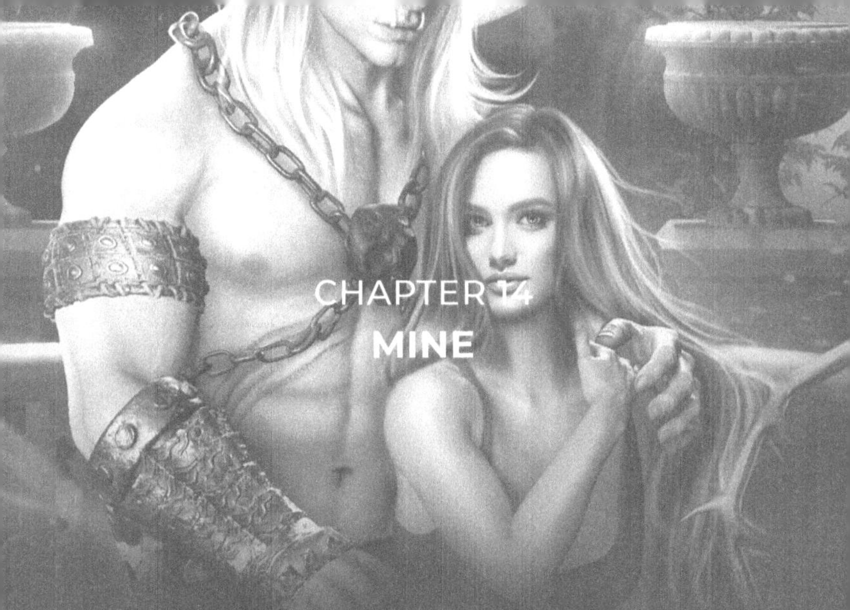

CHAPTER 14
MINE

HAURES

Three days later, I have cleared the castle of all soldiers. Dagon is traveling to Caol to report to the clan that he will no longer hunt for their village now that he is Susanna's personal guard. Castle staff have been warned to return to their quarters so that tonight is for their lord and his mate alone.

As I lead Susanna out to the scene I've prepared in the garden while she was curled up in the royal library earlier, I nod to see that it is also as empty as the rest of the palace had appeared.

"If anyone interrupts us this eve," I vow even so, "they will suffer the same fate as Bandu."

And Tropp, I think, though I don't add it. I never want Susanna to see my vengeance and mistake it for cruelty. I am ruthless, yes, and when it comes to my mate, anyone who even thinks to harm her will always perish. But I also refuse to frighten my mortal—who, after tonight, will be as immortal as I.

Still unfamiliar with how she can access my every want, my every thought, my every memory by using our bond, she has no idea what's passed through my mind. Even so, perfectly aware of what I have planned now that the gold moon has finally waned, my Su is in a cheerful mood.

Though, of course, that could've been because I propped her up on the library seat, *kiss*ing her cunt repeatedly after I found her reading earlier. I have been doing the same for days. I could not claim her with my cock, but my tongue and my fingers… she has denied me no intimate touch. For a fleeting moment, I wondered if her 'ditto' did not fulfill her mating vow, and whether or not the gods were punishing us with the mating sickness until she did so, but I don't believe that. My Susanna is eager for her male's touch. She searches it out, no fever necessary.

I have an ulterior motive, of course, apart from simply pleasuring her. Unlike other demons in Sombra, I do not have shadows. Therefore, I cannot change my shape. The cock that I have is what I must use on my wee mortal mate, and I haven't forgotten the look of surprise that crossed her beautiful face when she implored me to undress in front of her and share a steaming tub with her the first night I had her moved into my—our—quarters.

She tried wrapping her hands around it, making another strange human sound when it was a struggle for her to do so. And while Su has tiny hands, I am concerned that that means she also has a shallow cunt.

I will give her what I can. Anything to finalize our bond and claim my mate. Still, I want to make it pleasurable for her like any demon male would. So, learning how her body responds to her male, I've *kiss*ed her cunt, I've bitten off my claws and dipped my fingers inside her much cooler body, nearly spilling seed in my trousers when I imagined how it would feel when her slick, tight little form took as much of me as she can manage.

Which, should she welcome me tonight, will happen beneath the pale blue moon overhead...

So while I'm already imagining laying her out in the pile of bedding that they use out in the smaller villages, Susanna laughs as she thinks of me eliminating my demons all because they might interrupt our mating night.

She bumps her shoulder against my side, brushing up against the scars that I no longer see as a sign of weakness. Not when Susanna strokes them absently after we pleasure each other, telling me that she thinks it's 'hot' that I survived an arkoda without any help.

Of course it is 'hot'. The challenge between the

arkoda and I happened near the firepits of Sombra, after all…

Tiptoeing softly through the gardens, she sighs. "It's a beautiful night. Simply gorgeous."

Just like she is. "Yes."

"And you did this… for me?"

A rush of emotions soar down our bod. Ah, Su… my mate thinks me romantic—and she is as pleased as she is, like her male, anticipating what is to come.

I can't help myself. Tugging her close, pressing my mouth against hers, I rumble softly and admit, "For you, I try."

Once I've reluctantly released, her gaze lands on the nest waiting for us. "I see. I… so, um, I guess that's where we're going to do this? Huh?"

I reach out again, settling my palm on her shoulder. Her skin is so soft and warm and utterly *human*. It's nothing like mine. I'm made of calloused palms, corded strength, a brutal body, all horns and claw. I've killed for this female. If I had to end my existence for her, I would.

Without Susanna, there would *be* no existence left for Haures.

I stole the throne from Yelios, accepting and defeating any challenger to the throne. I've ruled over Sombra for two thousand years, making deals in the dark with the doppelseers. I am the most powerful demon in our realm—

—and, yet, I have never done anything so monumental as this.

My fingers tremble. That catches her attention, pulling her gaze toward me now.

Her brow furrows. "Haures? Hey. You alright?"

Am I?

"Susanna…" My voice is suddenly hoarse, tight with emotion. "I am trying not to scare you."

She snorts, her humor returning. "You can't."

I cock my head. "I can't?"

"Nope." She taps her chest, and my cock twitches to see her pat her luscious human breasts. "I've got the bond with you, remember? No matter what, if there's one thing I know about you? You won't let anyone hurt me. And that includes you."

"Yes," I breathe out. She does… she *does* understand. "I will never."

"I know." Taking her hand from her chest, she wraps it around my smallest finger. "And once I'm your bonded mate… once I'm immortal… you can stop worrying about that. Even then, I know you'll protect me."

"I vow it."

She raises one of the furry strips over her dim eyes. "Then prove it."

I want to. Desperately.

But—

"I don't know what I'm doing," I admit. "I've

never done this. Claiming a female… what if I do it wrong?"

Susanna's soft laughter is a balm to my jagged soul. "Haures, seriously? First of all, I know you're a virgin. Me, too. That's the best part of us doing this thing, the two of us. If we do it wrong, how will either of us know?" She gives my finger another tug. "Come with me," she says, echoing the same words I said to her when I released her from the dungeon, bringing her to the upper floors of the palace for the first time. "We'll learn together."

That's all the invitation I need. Well, apart from the delectable scent of her body readying itself for her male. She smells divine, and I know that her cunt's juices—along with the pleasure I've given her, and how deliberately I've been trying to stretch her out—will help ease my cock where it belongs.

Just on the edge of the bedding, I fall to my knees before her. After all, how else can I worship my mate properly if I don't do so?

With no one to spy on what we plan to do, Susanna doesn't just lift her skirts. She removes the entire dress, her pink skin glowing blue beneath the oasis's light. Her fingers grab my horns, guiding me as I kiss her thighs, her stomach, her hips… I taste her musk, her ice, and a hint of fire that tells me that even Susanna knows that she belongs to Sombra.

She belongs to *me*.

Releasing one horn, she threads her fingers

through my hair as I slowly kiss higher. Su knows what her mate desires. Spreading her thighs as far as she can, giving me space to wedge my big body between them, I mate her with my tongue until she's panting my name, legs trembling on either side of my face.

Only then do I believe that Susanna is ready to take her male.

It's easy to rise up even in this position, gathering her up on my shoulder so that I can carry her over to the bedding. Once I have laid her out, I remove my trousers so that I am as naked as she is.

Her small teeth dig into her bottom lip. Her eyes go wide. "Holy shit, Haures. I… crud. You're just so big everywhere."

"You can take me," I promise, and it is another vow. "You are my mate. You were made for me."

She nods. "Yes. Haures… yes. I am."

Again, it's an invitation that I would be a fool to ignore.

Still, I want to make sure that, before I claim her for all eternity, she has one last chance to deny me. "We don't have to do this tonight. We can wait. Just say the word, my love."

Her eyes glimmer as I call her what she's always been: *my love*.

"Say the word?" she whispers throatily, stroking the cords in my thick neck. "Okay. *Please*."

The last of any restraint I might've had *snaps*.

Bowing my head, I kiss her again. It's on the

mouth this time, swallowing her cries of pleasure mingled with slight pain as I feed my cock into Susanna's hungry cunt. There is resistance. I won't pretend there isn't. I go slow, easing my way in. I don't push. I go achingly slow, pausing when she bites my lip, the pain echoing down our band.

"This… this is enough," I tell her. "I can give you my seed, and we will be bonded."

Susanna shakes her head, dark hair splayed against the bedding. "No. I… you were right. I can take it. Just…" She scoots a little beneath me, adjusting her position. Panting softly, she grins up at me. "Okay. Keep going. I'm ready for you to fuck me."

Fuck me.

It's a human word for 'mate', and it hits me in this moment: this is the first time I have ever done this, but it is the same for Susanna. No other male has touched the inside of her cunt as I have.

The need to possess her completely overtakes her demon. I am no rogue. I do not lose all of my senses. And yet… it seems like I do as I pull out of her body, returning my cock to its grip before it can cool down again.

The more I thrust into my mate, the warmer she is. Her body is acclimating to mine in all ways. She is stretched around my length, taking me beautifully. Immortality is settling over her as well. She feels no pain now, only pleasure, as our temperatures slowly begin to match.

We are one. In every way that counts, we are one, and the mating vow has made it so that it will be forever.

And not even an ashbalm flower nor my powers will be enough to snap the bond that I have with my mate.

Thank the gods.

EPILOGUE

SUSANNA

FOUR DECADES LATER

The ashbalm flower works.

You would think that, after living by Haures's side for all these decades, I would've seen him use it. Not so. He might project himself as the ruthless, powerful, haughty ruler of our world, but I know better. There is no one in Sombra who understands the sanctity of the mate bond like our bondmaster.

True, there have been times when Haures sent some of our subjects into the shadows, searching for the flower. There was a young demon who thought he had made a mistake, bonding a Soleil demoness to him before his journey through the dark left him realizing how much he would risk to return to her. And, of course, there was Hope, a human woman—and Sammael's one true mate—that was sent on the same mission to repair their bond.

That was Sammael's fault. His innocent questions about the human world were not as innocent as they seemed, and his wayward obsession only grew until he managed to get his claws on the *Grimoire du Sombra*, casting the matefinder spell on his own, and becoming a phantom for a time in my old realm.

The other human-mate pairs each had their own unique troubles over the past few decades. Before I managed to convince Haures to let me go back for the spellbook—and he never did, sending Sammael to retrieve it instead… which, in hindsight, probably wasn't the smartest plan—another mortal read the spell.

My eight-year-old niece, Amelia.

All these years later, I still feel awful at how I reacted, though I wouldn't have changed a thing I did. At twenty-eight, I was more than ready to accept a demon mate. At *eight*? Amy was a child, and at my urging, Haures eventually gave Nox my old cell in the dungeon. By the time we knew that my young niece was the mortal mate that Nox was going off-plane to visit after she summoned him, Amy was twelve. Still way too young, and if I'm being honest, I don't know if I would've agreed to his release fourteen years later (when Amy was twenty-six) if Nox hadn't staged a dungeon-break himself.

That was, oh, two decades ago now. They are as happily mated as Haures and I still are, though Amy's path took a different direction from mine. I stayed in Sombra. Ever since Nox broke free to save her in a similar way that Haures once saved me, the newly bonded pair chose to stay in Connecticut, in my old house in Madison.

I gave it to her. I didn't know then that Mindy was still paying my mortgage on top of hers, as though she was sure I'd one day come home to it. My inheritance had paid for most of it, so the fee wasn't *that* much, and by the time Amy was an adult, it was paid up. Now it's hers, and I have the satisfaction of knowing that my niece is happy living with her mate in my old home. And Mindy? She's having a great life, even after all of the hardships she's been dealt.

It wasn't just me disappearing all those years ago, or how Haures's first law means that I could never let her know that I was okay. Mindy's not a mate. Amy is, so I only hope she found a way to ease my sister's sadness, but I wasn't the only one who vanished.

According to Amy, her father followed in her grandfather's footsteps. Within a year of me summoning Haures and going to stay in Sombra, Mindy and Dan were divorced. Her husband took off, quickly becoming estranged from both Mindy and Amy.

I didn't know then what caused it. Discovering recently that *Dan* was the 'something important' to me that Yelios kept in his keeping while waiting for my firstborn? During the final confrontation, when Haures, Amy, her mate, and I arrived in the shadows to help rescue a stolen child, it was Dan Dillon who was spit out of the shadows in exchange for Shannon and Malphas's infant daughter.

I had no idea. Hearing him babble about how he went to my house after my disappearance, plotting to steal my spellbook and sell it for cash before Yelios's shadows found him, snared him, and used him to do his bidding for nearly forty years… I should've felt remorse.

I didn't.

I never thought Yelios would be able to hurt me. In the last four decades, I've never left Mavro. Haures refused to allow it, and I wouldn't want to leave even if he did. I believed the ancient king couldn't reach across worlds—and, yes, I *was* wrong about that—and that by staying here, I was keeping everyone I cared about safe.

Though, if it came down to Yelios turning Dan into his puppet or him taking over either Mindy or Amy… I know who I would choose. I only hope that Dan appreciates that, even now, Haures is willing to show mercy when I ask for it. Instead of leaving Dan to slowly lose his mind in the shadows, he brought me back to Mavro, then returned to retrieve my brother-in-law.

For the last few weeks, he's been the new occupant of the cell that, so long ago, once was mine. Between students from the School of Mages casting their spells over him, and a sweet demoness willing to watch over the addled human male, they're trying to break Yelios's hold on him. The only hold left is one of Dan's making. Yelios might have used another demon's essence to bond Dan to him as his servant, but when Yelios finally moved on, his tie to my brother-in-law ended. He should recover in time, but if he doesn't…

At least Amy will know that I tried.

For Mindy's sake, I should've abandoned him. If it were up to the human mother of the kidnapped child, she would've used Glaine's sword to lop off Dan's head. But Amy… she understands why I stole her mate from her for so long and doesn't hold it against me. Still, if I can return her father to her, maybe we can all start over.

The prophecy that has been hanging over my mate's head for more than two thousand years has finally come to pass. And after it was over? I understood why Bandu was so certain that I would inevitably lead to the end of Sombra to the point that he was willing to kill me—and then died for it.

Alana was the half-human, half-demon child spoken of in the prophecy. However, if I had never found the spellbook… if I had never worked so hard to translate it… if I had never left my notes in the margin so that Shannon, Alana's mother, could summon Malphas, her father, leading the two of them to create the child…

Yelios claimed that he knew what would happen in the future. He believed that the child spoken of in the prophecy would be his lost mate returned to him; she was even given the same name, though Malphas did it in honor of the queen, not that she was Alana reborn. But he believed that Haures and I would be the parents of that child. That's why he made me promise to give up my firstborn all those years ago, and why my mate and I have spent the last four decades without starting a family of our own.

I was the first human mate, but I wasn't the only one. It could've been Amy, but before I could warn her of her fate should she get pregnant, she made the decision on her own not to have any children for the time being.

But Shannon did, and the prophecy was set into motion.

It's over now. Once upon a time, I looked at the promise of my happy-ever-after with Haures and agreed to start over. With Yelios gone, and Sombra saved until the doppelseers have another vision of our end, this… this is a new beginning.

Our new beginning.

And, to me, it's fitting that it starts on the night of the gold moon…

Things have been so hectic. As much as I was happy to see Dagon find his mate in Sierra, I have to admit, I would've preferred his company to the young guard that has served as my bodyguard in the cycles since Dagon moved to stay with Sierra in the human world.

Lyre is a bit jumpy for a soldier, and I know that Haures gave him to my keeping because, otherwise, Glaine was prepared to send him away from the guards' barracks on the outskirts of Mavro. Still, he's devoted and determined to keep the duchess safe, even though there hasn't been another attempt on my life since Bandu.

Mainly because Haures let it be known that, to challenge me, was to end up as ash, just like the seer.

I am Sombra's biggest open secret, amused every time I meet another demon who doesn't know that Haures has a human woman for a mate. If my very mortal name spelled out on his chest in silver ink wasn't a clue, the fact that he's been more prone to show me over the last decade or so should've been. It doesn't matter.

Yelios is gone.

The threat to our firstborn child is over.

And Haures… my demon duke has the one thing he's always wanted apart from his mate.

He has *shadows*.

I like to think that that was a parting gift from Yelios to Haures. When my mate used his special gift as the bondmaster—plus the ashbalm flower that Shannon plucked in the dark woods while searching for her missing child—to break the last remnants of the bond between Queen Alana and King Yelios that kept him trapped here, Yelios released his hold on the shadows.

I guess the excess needed to go somewhere. Haures got the bulk of them, with Amy's mate, Nox, accepting the rest. Now Haures can finally change shapes, heal, and carry me off into the night's sky with the dual moons as our backdrop. And Nox? His stay in the dungeon—and subsequent breakout—left him damaged. Yelios's shadows made him whole again.

Though, sometimes, I think that it wasn't really the shadows that did. Same for Haures. I always thought it was so coincidental that, like me, Amy was meant for a Sombra demon. That the book found her, even though she went looking for it first, and that the magic worked despite how young she was.

After my niece returned to the human world with Nox once Yelios was defeated, I've thought of it even more. And I've decided that, for some reason, we *were* both meant for Sombra demons in need. Like us Benoit women were made to bond two broken males, love them, and make them whole.

Nox spent fourteen years in the dungeon. Haures

spent two thousand years in a prison of his own making, taking the throne from Yelios because he knew he'd have a mate, and that her arrival would herald everything that happened leading up to the prophecy (and, well, *did*).

I was able to bond with Haures despite him having no shadows. Amy was strong enough to accept Nox as her mate when only a drop of his essence remained. It was Fate, and I've never been more content in my decision to choose Haures and promise myself to him than I am tonight.

Every day, I love him more. Whether he wears the crystal crown, sits on the throne, or can change to shadows now… he's my mate, and when I want him, all I have to do is tug on our bond.

The familiar white orb *pops* into existence. A moment later, Haures—with his inky-black skin, beautiful blue eyes, and dark hair that will become pale again once he turns solid—appears in our bedroom.

His feet touch the tile, instantly returning to the form I know so well and absolutely adore.

He crosses his arms over his chest, looking down at me with a hungry expression. "Su?"

"Mm," is my non-committal answer.

What else do I have to say?

I'm stretched out on our bed, gloriously naked. The book I'd asked Billie—Glaine's brash yet kind mate—to borrow from Shannon's Earth Library the last time she visited Nuit is perched by my side. It's a modern romance, where the human woman mates with a monster, and though I probably summoned my mate out of an important meeting in his throne room, I don't care.

I need him. And when I need Haures, all I have to do is call.

Besides, the gold moon is out. Everyone in Sombra knows not to disturb a bonded pair when the gold moon is out.

For forty years, we had to be careful. While we could pleasure each other in every way that exists—and, after four decades, we former virgins might've figured them all out—to keep from getting pregnant with a child that the gods would make me give to Yelios due to my vow, intercourse was a no-go. If he put his cock anywhere near my pussy during the night of the gold moon, I'd get pregnant instantly.

Ask Shannon. Ask Kennedy. Ask Sierra, who doesn't know it yet, but is carrying my future niece or nephew since Dagon is basically my brother…

And tonight?

It's finally my turn.

And I know *exactly* what to say.

"Haures," I whisper throatily, unable to hide my smile. I might look like twenty-eight-year-old Susanna Benoit. Thanks to the gift of immortality that comes with mating a Sombra demon, I feel like it, too. But with four decades of love and affection and memories between us, when I say, "Please," he knows what I mean.

He is my demon duke.

I am his duchess.

And, tonight, we'll finally take the next step in adding to our happily-ever-after: a child of our own, conceived on the night of the gold moon.

I can't friggin' wait.

AUTHOR'S NOTE

And there you have it! It's short and it's sweet and it ended with a bang (literally), but now you know how Susanna and Haures ended up happily mated!

It's bittersweet, closing out the series with the couple that—technically—began it all, but this isn't the end for Sombra! Don't forget, the next gen spin-off begins with Alana's romance, *Tell Them That I'm Coming*.

After that? Well, I'll might be delving into a different sort of monster next year.

Frost giants and ancient warriors and mate auctions sound like fun?

Until then, my eternal thanks for you taking all these trips with me to Sombra, and I can't wait until we can do it again!

xoxo,

Sarah

PRE-ORDER NOW

TELL THEM THAT I'M COMING

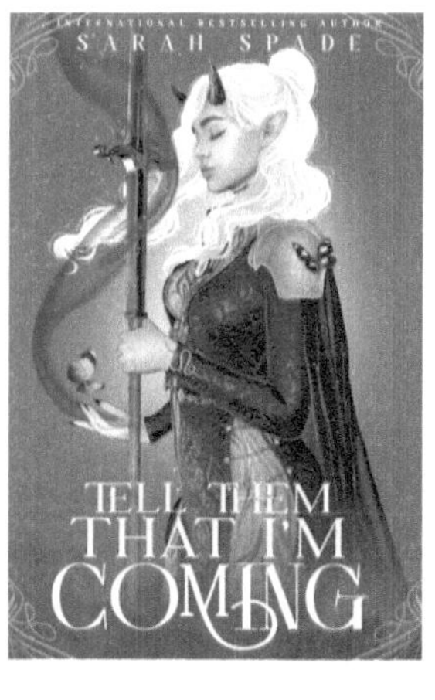

My destiny was never mine to begin with...

I swear, if I never heard the word 'prophecy' again, it'll be too soon.

My whole life, I've know that I was the child of prophecy. Half-human, half-demon, I was only four months old when I supposedly saved the world. Twenty-five years later, I strive to have a future when I've already done what I was born to do.

And that's when I overhear my parents discussing a *second* prophecy about me...

Each halfling in Sombra has their own gift. Mine has been my ability to wield the shadows that make up my father's home world. Along with my soul-pet, Binx, and my best friend, Rafe, I can visit all of the neighboring realms.

Except for one.

Noctavara isn't home to demons. The human realm has no contact with the warded world, either. It's a gilded cage for the fae—and the plane where I'm meant to find my future.

But, first, I have to find *Rafe.*

Sold to a slaver in Noctavara, I'm determined to get him back any way I can… which would be a lot easier if I didn't get caught by a fae bandit who has his own reasons to help me reach the Gilded Court.

And me? When I realize who he is, I have my own reasons to escape his golden gaze and blinding smile… but Thane Aurex is more *persuasive* than he should be, and now Binx and I had a new fae companion.

As we journey together through a world unlike the one I left behind, I have one message for the cruel court that thinks they can steal from Alana of Sombra:

Tell them that I'm coming.

Alana of Sombra.

The prophecy warned her that she'd find her future in Noctavara.

The prophecy forgot to mention that she'd have to find her way there first—or that she would be captured by Thane Aurex while on a journey to save her best friend from the Gilded Court...

Tell Them That I'm Coming is a romantasy starring Malphas and Shannon's daughter, Alana, and the mysterious fae she can't help but be drawn to—even if his people are cursed never to have a mate.

PRE-ORDER NOW

FROM PLAYING DEAD TO TRYING TO KEEP FROM MAKING THAT STATE PERMANENT...

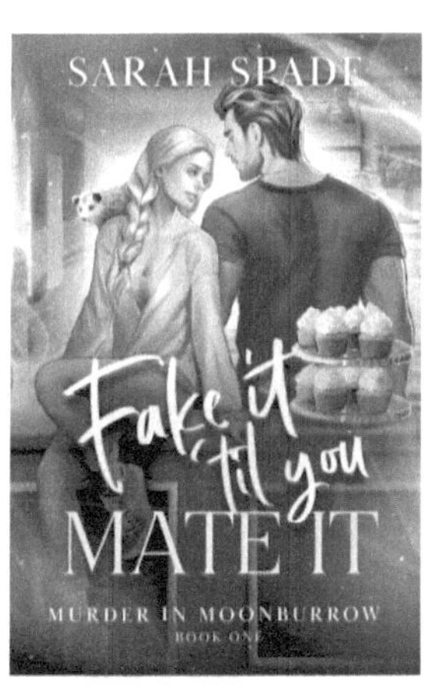

WHEN I WAKE UP IN THE MORGUE, I KNOW IT'S TIME TO MOVE ON...

When people think of shifters, they always bring up the predators: wolves, bears, big cats. But prey shifters exist, too; the bunnies, the hedgehogs, and my old childhood nemesis, Roxy, who was an adorable raccoon and a huge headache.

Then there's me. Honey Morgan, one in a long line of Virginia opossums—and who has a tendency to 'play dead' at the worst possible moments.

For nearly my whole life, I've managed to live

among humans who have no clue that I'm a supe. But when I get startled and drop only to wake up in the *morgue*, I have to admit my mother was right: us opossums need to be around other shifters, even if the local predators have me hissing.

Or maybe that's just one.

Max Lobo. To the outsiders who pass through Moonburrow, he is the scowly sheriff. To the supe residents, he is the all-powerful Alpha of the Moonshadow Pack.

To me? He's my *mate*.

He doesn't seem to recognize me as his, though, and I'm okay with that. After all, I'm too busy taking over my witchy grandmother's old bakery. With her recipes, my sense of humor and work ethic, and my mother's support from across the world, I focus on making Dough You Believe In Magic a success.

Which probably would've been a lot easier if I didn't stumble upon a dead predator outside my back door—or if it didn't bring the Alpha to my front one.

Thrown together with Max, I have to figure out who targeted my bakery, why it seems like I might've been the one they were after, and how to survive being around the Alpha as he begins to realize that I'm not just some newcomer prey bumbling around on his territory that he needs to protect… but the other half of his wolf's soul he has to claim.

Hey. Fake it 'til you mate it, right?

KEEP IN TOUCH

Stay tuned for what's coming up next! Follow me at any of these places—or sign up for my newsletter—for news, promotions, upcoming releases, and more!

SarahSpadeBooks.com
Sarah's Newsletter
Sarah's Signed Book Store

facebook.com/sarahspadebooks
x.com/stressie
instagram.com/sarahspadebooks
amazon.com/author/sarahspade

ALSO BY SARAH SPADE

Murder in Moonburrow

Fake It 'Til You Mate It

Play Dead, Stay Dead

Of Magic and Murder

Holiday Hunk

Halloween Boo

This Christmas

Auld Lang Mine

I'm With Cupid

Getting Lucky

When Sparks Fly

Holiday Hunk: the Complete Series

Claws and Fangs

Leave Janelle

Never His Mate

Always Her Mate

Forever Mates

Hint of Her Blood

Taste of His Skin

Stay With Me

Never Say Never: Gem & Ryker

Bound by the Moon

Sombra Demons

Drawn to the Demon Duke*

Mated to the Monster

Stolen by the Shadows

Santa Claws

Bonded to the Beast

Fated to the Phantom

Claimed by the Creature

Grabbed by the Guard

Taken by the Twins

Shannon in Sombra

Stolen Mates

The Alpha's Heart*

The Feral's Captive

Chase and the Chains

The Beta's Bride

Wolves of Winter Creek

Prey

Pack

Predator

Protector

Sanctuary

Watch Me Burn

Make Me Bleed

Claws Clause

(written as Jessica Lynch)

Mates **free*

Hungry Like a Wolf

Of Mistletoe and Mating

No Way

Season of the Witch

Rogue

Sunglasses at Night

Ain't No Angel

True Angel

Ghost of Jealousy

Night Angel

Broken Wings

Of Santa and Slaying

Lost Angel

Born to Run

Uptown Girl

A Pack of Lies

Here Kitty, Kitty

Ordinance 7304: the Bond Laws (Claws Clause Collection #1)

Living on a Prayer (Claws Clause Collection #2)

Diamonds are a Witch's Best Friend (Claws Clause Collection #3)

www.ingramcontent.com/pod-product-compliance
Lightning Source LLC
Chambersburg PA
CBHW031042310726
48969CB00007B/2079

* 9 7 8 1 9 6 1 5 9 4 4 6 3 *